POSH
AND PREJUDICE

POSH
AND PREJUDICE

by Grace Dent

poppy

LITTLE, BROWN AND COMPANY
New York   Boston

Poppy

Hachette Book Group
237 Park Avenue, New York, NY 10017
For more of your favorite series, visit our website at www.pickapoppy.com

Poppy is a imprint of Little, Brown and Company.
The Poppy name and logo are trademarks of Hachette Book Group, Inc.

First Edition: December 2009

First published in Great Britain in 2007 by Hodder Children's Books,
a division of Hachette Children's Books

The characters and events portrayed in this book are fictitious. Any similarity to
real persons, living or dead, is coincidental and not intended by the author.

Library of Congress Cataloging-in-Publication Data
Dent, Grace.
　　Posh and prejudice / by Grace Dent. — 1st ed.
　　　　p. cm.
　　"Poppy."
　　Sequel to: Diary of a chav.
　　Summary: At the end of her last year of compulsory education, sixteen-year-old
Shiraz resigns herself to life in her gritty London suburb, serving fried eggs at
Mr. Yolk and dating plumber-in-training Wesley, until she receives high marks in
her examinations and decides to enroll in her school's "Center of Excellence"
program.
　　ISBN 978-0-316-03484-5
　　[1. Self-realization — Fiction.　2. Social classes — Fiction.　3. Schools —
Fiction.　4. Diaries — Fiction.　5. England — Fiction.]　I. Title.
　　PZ7.D4345Po 2009
　　[Fic—]DC22

　　　　　　　　　　　　　　　　　　　　　　　　　　　　　　2008043853

10 9 8 7 6 5 4 3 2 1

RRD-C

Printed in the United States of America

For Miss Ruby Chaisty

This diary belongs to:

Shiraz Bailey Wood

Address: 34, THUNDERSLEY ROAD,
Goodmayes,
Essex,
IG5 2XS

AUGUST

TUESDAY 19TH AUGUST

I am the master of my own destiny.

Well, that's what Ms. Bracket, my English teacher last year, always says.

"Shiraz Bailey Wood," she says. "The sky is the limit for a bright spark like you! You could be anything you want. Like an astronaut! Or a lion tamer! Or the Prime Minister! The only thing stopping you is yourself!"

She used to jar my head sometimes she did. She was proper obsessed about us passing our GCSEs. Ms. Bracket isn't bothered about all that "Superchav Academy" stuff. That's what a lot of snobby newspaper reporters used to call my old school Mayflower Academy, you see. And I'll say it again for the billionth time . . .

WE WEREN'T ALL CHAVS, RIGHT!?

(Jury's out on Uma Brunton-Fletcher, though.)

Ms. Bracket isn't prejudiced and stigmatizing toward young people like most grown-ups are. Saying that, she doesn't take any of our crap either. Like when I told her me and Carrie didn't need no English GCSEs 'cos we were starting a world-famous singing duo called Half Rice/Half Chips.

"Fair enough, Shiraz," Ms. Bracket says. "But in the event that you *don't* become the next Beyoncé Knowles you'll need to get a job to feed and clothe yourself! SO DO YOUR HOMEWORK!"

In the end even I had to admit that passing my GCSEs was a better plan if I didn't want to end up flogging the homeless paper *Street News* outside Food Lion. If you've ever seen that YouTube clip of me and Carrie on ITV2's *Million Dollar Talent Show* you'll know why. Oh my days, that was well shameful.

Ten pounds flaming ninety-two pence we spent on those matching red leg warmers and devil horns, then we only get one verse into "Maneater" by Nelly Furtado and this snotty-looking judge in trousers so tight you could see the outline of his trouser-snake tells me I'm singing like someone strangling a donkey.

Yeah, BARE JOKES, bruv. Jog on.

Not like I cared though. I just laughed in his face. He was like thirty-three years old or something. A proper antique. It's not my fault if he couldn't appreciate me being an individual.

Oh well, that's break over. Better get back to work.

2:15PM — I don't regret nothing in my life. Nothing. I'm always moving forward, me. I'm keeping it real. It's just sometimes, when I'm standing here behind this pan, frying an egg, and I'm proper sweaty and some bloke with a hairy bum cleavage is at the counter moaning on going, "Ugggh, you've made my yolk hard. I wanted it runny. I like my eggs runny!" . . . Well, it's times like that when I remember Mayflower Academy. I think about what a laugh Year Eleven was with Carrie and Luther and Chantalle and Uma and Kezia.

Y'know there was a bit last year when I even started planning to go to Sixth Form. And I ain't exactly a Sixth Formery type of girl if you know what I mean.

But I never thought I'd wind up here at Mr. Yolk on Goodmayes High Street making Set Breakfast C two hundred times a day for geezers with bigger baps than me.

This was NOT in Shiraz Bailey Wood's life plan.

"EAT LIKE A PRINCE FOR £2!!" That's the "mission statement" at Mr. Yolk. It's written in BIG CAPITAL LETTERS across the front of my T-shirt. I know I look totally butterz in it, but my boyfriend, Wesley Barrington Bains II, says I look hot.

"Wifey," Wesley says. "You could put on anything and you'd look buff, innit."

Wesley reckons I've got it proper cushy working at Mr. Yolk 'cos:

1) It's just down the road from my mother's house, and
2) I get free dinner every day and they do steak and kidney pot pies, and
3) He can pop in and see me on the way to his plumbing NVQ and get his egg roll.

Wesley don't like his egg runny. Wesley likes his egg yolk quite hard and he likes the ketchup just on the egg white NOT the yolk, with a sprinkle of black pepper on the yolk. The first dozen times I made Wesley's egg I got it wrong, but now I make Wesley's egg just perfect he reckons. That's my biggest achievement all August.

I'm dreading picking up my GCSE results next week. I tried my best and everything. I knew that *Jane Eyre* book backward by May! I used to go to sleep at night and dream about Mr. Rochester on his horse, clip-clopping through Romford and scooping me up outside Time and Envy nightclub and taking me away from Essex.

I tried my total best in that exam, honest.

It wouldn't be the first time my best wasn't good enough.

WEDNESDAY 20TH AUGUST

Oh my gosh, today at Mr. Yolk was proper DULL. OK. I tell a lie, there was one exciting bit at about 3 o'clock when we totally ran out of one-quid coins and Mario (Mr. Yolk himself — Goodmayes's biggest celebrity) let me get the bus to the bank in Ilford Mall and get some.

So I take one of my detours round by Greggs the bakers and I spot Kezia Marshall and we both buy a gingerbread man in the shape of Bart Simpson. Then we sit on the wall outside Claire's Accessories chatting about Kezia's bump. Last year everyone thought Kezia was pregnant by Luther — then it turned out to be a false alarm. Then it didn't. Kezia really was pregnant by Luther. Even my mum was shocked at that.

Kezia's bump is well big now. She looks like one of them Tele-tubbies with her red hair and orange hoodie and big belly. Like LaLa or Tinky Winky, me and Carrie couldn't decide. Kezia kept pulling down the front of her trackie pants and making me feel the bump kicking. Kezia didn't mind which passersby saw the bump and pretty much all the rest of her downstairs bits too. (Safe to say, red is Kezia's natural hair color.) I didn't feel like my gingerbread man much after that. I worry about Kezia a bit. Kezia says Luther ain't calling her much no more like he used to. Kezia says all their mums and dads are trying to sort something out. Poor Kez.

I asked about baby names and Kezia says she likes Usher for a boy or Latanoyatiqua for a girl. Then she's going to double-barrel the surnames. Latanoyatiqua Marshall-Dinsdale! Oh my days — by the time the poor kid's got that spelled in finger paints at school the day will be over.

I went back to Mr. Yolk and Mario was all up in my face giving it. "Where you been? I give you ten minutes!" So I said I had menstrual pain in my womb and had been in Boots looking at the ladies intimate problem counter, then Mario pushed away his beans on toast and made a face like "Too much information" and got back on the phone to his bookie.

See, even the exciting bits at work ain't that exciting. Only fifty more years and I can retire.

8PM — My mother — Mrs. Diane Wood — says work ain't meant to be exciting. Mum reckons the important thing is that I'm bringing home some cash and earning my keep. This ALONE should be exciting enough for me, Mum reckons. Yeah, she is barking mad. I love my mother 'cos like you have to don't you, but she is a proper mental sometimes when she says stuff like this.

I said to her, "Mother, have you ever cleaned out a deep fat fryer and had your bum cheek pinched by an eighty-six-year-old customer with missing bottom teeth for £3.50 an hour?!! It AIN'T EXCITING, right?"

"Oh, Shiraz. Give it a rest. Real life ain't never exciting." My mother sighed. She was half-staring at *Emmerdale,* where some vet had his arm up a cow's bumhole. "REAL LIFE AIN'T NEVER EXCITING!" my mum said again. "That's why I pay for this bleeding Sky+ satellite TV subscription!"

I gave her £50 out of my wages toward my keep and she rolled it up and stuck it in her pocket. Then she rubbed Penny, our obese Staffy, and said, "Woohoo Pennywenny! More Russell Stover Chocolates for you and me. Ooh, we like those coffee truffle ones, don't we?!"

She'd better be joking.

I went to my room and put cotton balls in my ears to drown out the noise and carried on with this book I'm reading called *Pride and Prejudice* by a bird called Jane Austen. Ms. Bracket said I would like it and I do. It's proper old. It's about this woman called Elizabeth who fancies this well-minted proper buff bloke called Darcy who is sexy but up himself. I can't stand lads like that.

10PM — Carrie just texted. Carrie's going to schlep over tomorrow and do me some false nails. Carrie says she's going to use some stronger glue this time. Carrie says she's still a bit freaked out about the last time she did them. One of them fell off at work when I was making the tuna mayo and Mario had to give some old geezer the Heimlich maneuver when it got jammed in his windpipe. That was definitely exciting. Just, like, not in a good way.

THURSDAY 21ST AUGUST

This house is driving me MAD. You never get a minute of peace unless you actually get into your bed then pull the duvet over your head and shut your eyes and even then my gigantic little brother Murphy will be poking the duvet saying, "'Ere Shizza, the toaster's got all black smoke coming out of it. Is it meant to do that?" Or my mother will be in my room going, "Ooh, lying down are we? All right for some! It's your turn to pick up the dog turds in the back garden. I'll get you the shovel!"

34 Thundersley Road is always proper hectic. Especially when me and my mum and my dad and Murphy and my big sister Cava-Sue and her bloke Lewis and my bloke Wesley are all in at the same time. Nan comes round a lot too. And sometimes she brings her mate Clement from bingo.

Dad says he's thinking of installing a ticket system on the loo door like at the ShopRite deli counter so he stands a chance of taking a dump. We all laughed our heads off when he said that 'cept Mum who told him to stop being so filthy. My dad don't say much but when he does he is bare jokes.

There was a bit last year where our Cava-Sue got well rinsed out with Thundersley Road and was proper sick of sharing a bedroom with me and sick of our bunkbeds and sick of Mum bending her ear about her looking all emo and sick of Goodmayes altogether so she did a runner to London. But me and Mum really missed her so I got us all on the TV show *Fast-Track Family Feud* and got her back.

Yeah, good idea, Shiz.

I didn't know two months later she'd move her flipping boyfriend in here too!

"Lewis's mother Vera is moving to Benidorm!" Cava-Sue says last February. "She's setting up an English lesbian mock-Tudor theme pub called the Fistwell Inn and making my Lewis homeless! She says Lewis can fend for himself! Can you belieeeeeve it? He's only nineteen! What's he going to dooooo??!"

No sooner had Cava-Sue begun hinting loudly that she was

moving out again to be with Lewis than the floppy-haired emo git had moved his collection of thrift shop shirts, ties, and nose rings into our house.

I was turfed out of the room me and Cava-Sue used to share. Then Mum dispatched Dad off to Home Depot to buy some plasterboard and Murphy's room was halved in two with plasterboard and me and Murph both got half a room each. I still ain't seen the funny side and I don't care who knows it.

"I don't know what's wrong with your mush!" Cava-Sue said tonight when we were making food. "You always used to jar my bloody head in that bottom bunk about not having your own space!"

This made me proper angry. "Yeah, fair play, Cava-Sue," I said to her. "But now I'm living in a three-by-four square plasterboard space with no bleeding windows! There's geezers in that Abu Ghraib terrorist compound who see more daylight than I do! I ain't happy!"

"Oh, you're so bleeding dramatic! It's not forever! Me and Lewis are going traveling soon, remember!" Cava-Sue sighed, poking a Linda McCartney vegetarian sausage with a spatula.

"DRAMATIC!?" I shouted. "Maybe if your bed was separated from Murphy's by a two-inch-thick piece of posh cardboard and you could hear him grunting his bleeding way through *Nuts* magazine you'd feel bleeding DRAMATIC too!"

That well shut her up.

10PM — My best friend Carrie just came round and did my and Cava-Sue's nails. She did mine hot pink with acrylic tips and did Cava-Sue's dark purple. Carrie says I look well pretty with mine all long and that I'm looking proper womanly nowadays. Carrie says no wonder Wesley Barrington Bains II talks about marrying me one day. Carrie says I'm proper lucky to have found true love and know someone will love me forever. I suppose I am.

Carrie says she's well bored hanging about the house with her mother, Maria, and she wishes she had a job too. I said I'd ask Mr. Yolk if he needed anyone to help fry eggs.

" 'Ere don't be daft, Shiz," Carrie said. "Once the GCSE results are out next week we'll be going back to Sixth Form, right?!" Bless her. We are so NOT going to Sixth Form. She is proper delusional.

All I remember about the English Writing to Argue, Explain, or Advise GCSE Paper is spending three hours trying to convince folk — over a load of different exercises — that the theme parks of Florida were a steaming good place to go on holiday.

I mean, fair enough, I know I did better than Kezia Marshall 'cos when I looked over at Kezia fifteen minutes into Paper One, I swear she was coloring in a doodle she'd done of a stroller. But I don't think I did brilliant. The whole thing was a proper stress-out and the faster I wrote the more I began to get proper mixed-up and think bleeding hell I don't know if I'm putting apostrophes in the right place or using commas right or nothing. And all I seemed to keep saying was that dolphins were well good fun to swim with and by the time the bell went off I'd begun to think that I weren't even spelling the word dolphin right and I could feel my throat and my eyes beginning to hurt like I wanted to cry.

But I didn't cry 'cos I never ever cry in front of no one at school and I weren't bloody going to start then.

Carrie said that in her exam paper she didn't even argue that Florida was that good or nothing 'cos she went once with Barney and Maria in Year Eight and it wasn't no way as good as Dominican and the only thing she remembers was that there was tons of mosquitos at Wacky Water World and one of them bit her on the lady garden.

I said, " 'Ere, Carrie, you never wrote that in the exam did you?" and Carrie says, "Yeah, course I did, Shizza. I was keeping it real."

We are DOOMED.

FRIDAY 22ND AUGUST

So I got home from work tonight and gave my hair a lather-rinse-repeat-wash to get out all the smell of fry grease and I began ironing it straight and putting on some blusher and finding my charm bracelet when my mum shouts, "Wooooo-hoooo, Shiraz, LOVER BOY is here!" So I go look out of Cava-Sue's bedroom window and Wesley is outside parking up his banana-yellow Golf.

He gets out of the car and he's got on his black Kappa trackie pants and his navy Hackett sweatshirt and his pink Hackett shirt underneath and his hair's got styling wax in it like he always does when it's the weekend and he's proper making an effort. I watch him lock up the Golf, turn to walk away, then turn around and check it out for a bit, then walk back to it and examine a mark on the hood. Wesley loves his car.

My stomach still feels a bit funny when I see Wesley. Not as much as it used to when I first ever met him, but I still reckon he's buff and all that in his own way. He's a well lovely person too. And it's not like everyone can go out with someone proper choong like Ashton Kutcher can they?

Everyone in my house loves Wesley. The minute he walks in our house my mother — who can be a right old puffadder — is up making him a cup of tea and my dad is asking him what he reckons about the new West Ham soccer trade and my brother is trying to get him to play *Decapitation Nation* on PS2 and even Cava-Sue takes her clonking great clown's feet off the sofa and lets him park his bum.

"'Ere, Wesley, you couldn't have a look at our khazi could you?!" my mum was shouting through from the kitchen as I came downstairs. "It ain't filling right up when you flush!"

"Mother! Wesley don't wanna look at our khazi!" I said, looking around for my other hoop earring.

"Oh, I don't mind, innit," Wesley said smiling. "I got some tools in the trunk too if need be."

"In the trunk, Wesley!?" shouted Mum. "You don't wanna be carrying those tools round with you in yer trunk! They'll get stolen round 'ere."

"Well he never knows when he'll need them, Mum," I said, trying not to sound narky. "He never knows when we might have a bloody toilet emergency." Wesley laughed and started to go upstairs.

"'Ere, Wesley love, do you want a sandwich?" shouted Mum. "I got a can of corned beef opened here for the dog."

"Nah, Mrs. W!" shouted Wesley. "I'm taking Shiraz for some nosh before we go to the AMC Loews, innit."

"Oooh! Out for a meal!?" gasped my mum. "Very posh. 'Ere, you've got a good one there, Shiraz! I never got taken for no food when I was courting, did I, Brian? You never bought me a meal."

"You'd never have shut up long enough to eat it," muttered my dad from behind his *Daily Star*.

"What's that?" shouted my mother.

"I said, I was so in love I never felt like eating," said my dad.

After half an hour of Wesley crouching in our bathroom with his head in the toilet tank we finally left.

Me and Wesley went to Shanghai Shanghai in Romford Plaza for the All You Can Eat buffet, then we went to see *TurboChase Terror II* starring The Rock and Carmen Electra. The movie was about some geezer who had stolen a diamond but he didn't know he'd stolen it until he was being chased by The Rock and was being propositioned by Carmen Electra who spent the whole of the film lying about on car hoods wearing tops that didn't fit her. I didn't really want to watch *TurboChase Terror II,* but Wesley was proper keen. I wanted to watch this film called *The Magician's Maze* that I saw a thing about on telly the other night. It's about these kids who are left to run the world after a big nuclear war. Proper creepy it looked. But Wesley saw on the poster that it had subtitles and he was like no way.

"Aw, Shiz, I just wanna watch something. I don't wanna read too, innit," he said, when we were choosing our buffet. "I don't wanna feel like I'm back at school."

"Oh . . . S'alright," I said. "I ain't bothered." I tried to pull my face like I wasn't bothered but Wesley could see I was a bit so he paid the extra two quid a head so I could eat stuff from the duck section.

Like I say, he's well lovely like that, is my Wesley.

MONDAY 25TH AUGUST

Today was PROPER WEIRD.

On Mondays Mario always gets obsessed with bleaching the teacups. Don't flaming ask me why. He seems to think it's well important that the clientele always get a proper sparkling white teacup, when obviously BACK IN THE REAL WORLD it totally isn't. Half the geezers who come in Mr. Yolk for Set Breakfast C wouldn't give a monkey's if you served them tea in one of my Nan's old fluffy slippers with a corn bandage that fell off in the toe. They ain't fussy. But I don't argue with Mr. Yolk as to be honest it's quite nice having a bit of time out back faffing about with my yellow rubber gloves on, listening to KISS 100.

So anyway, it's 10AM and I'm at the sink up to my elbows in Clorox when Mario comes in and he goes, "Hey Shirelle, your little friend is here to see you." So I'm like, "Which one?" And he goes "One with all pink mouth and surprise face," so I know right away he means Carrie 'cos Mario has never understood what's going on with Carrie's eyebrows, which she plucks into proper thin arches these days.

Carrie has been really experimenting with her look ever since she got this book for Christmas called *Butterz to Babe in Thirty Days!* by this girl called Tabitha Tennant from Dagenham who got kicked out of *Big Brother* for cheating but now runs a beauty academy in Covent Garden in London. Tabitha is Carrie's heroine. Tabitha is the woman who started off the "cupid-bow" lips trend this summer where you paint your lipstick on in hot pink in dramatic arches like a doll. Carrie does that a lot at the moment.

So I take off my gloves and come through and right enough there's Carrie all made up, cupid-bow lips, two tone eye shadow, wearing a stripy off-the-shoulder top with a pink bra strap showing and jeans and big hoops looking like she's off to a club in Romford to see DJ Platinum. She looks at me and pulls a proper annoyed face and goes, "Shizza, are you mental or something?"

And I'm like, "What?" and she's like, "You were supposed to be taking this morning off! I been calling your phone since 8AM? Why you not showing me no love?"

So I go, "I've been frying eggs, you clown, I'm at work."

Carrie laughs and says, "I know you're at work, but you're supposed to be picking up your GCSE results!" and suddenly I remember and I feel all sick and proper anxious again just like when I finished the English exam and looked back through all that crap I'd scribbled about the dolphins.

"Oh God, yeah," I said to her. "I've been blocking it out mentally." Carrie just shook her head and sighed.

"Oh come on, Shiz," she said quite impatiently. "I wanna know what we got."

"But I'm busy," I mumbled, "I'm bleaching cups."

"Mmm . . . yeah, whatever," said Carrie. "Leave it to me."

Then Carrie wandered over to Mario who was sitting in the corner studying the racing section of the *Sun* with a pen in his mouth.

"Mr. Yolk?" Carrie said, making her voice even softer and tilting her head to the side. "Mario?"

"What you want, sweetheart?" he said.

"Mario? Is it OK if I borrow Shizza for a while? She has a doctor's appointment that she's clean forgotten about. I said I'd go with her . . . for moral support . . ." Carrie was doing a loud whisper now, "Shiraz is a bit EMBARRASSED to ask you, y'know? It's one of those *downstairs* things."

Carrie pointed in the region of her thong.

"Downstairs?" said Mario, then his face proper crumpled, "Oh . . . Go! You women and your bits. It never end. I have enough of you. You got an hour. Then Shirelle she come back and do lunch busy time. Go!"

I grabbed my pink hoodie and pulled it on over my apron and we skipped out of the door.

"I can't bloody believe that always works," I said to Carrie.

"I know, why do men always fall for that?" Carrie laughed. "That Mr. Cleaver who did gym at Mayflower actually thought I was on the blob four times a month." We both laughed well loud then 'cos just the thought of it was bare jokes.

Me and Carrie got the bus down to Mayflower Academy, listening to the new Dizzee Rascal on her Nokia and eating Whoppers which to be honest felt like stones in my gob 'cos I was feeling proper nervous. When we got to school we had to go to the brand new assembly hall which had just been re-opened after the fire at Christmas. We got in the line for our results. Everywhere you looked there was all my old year with cells clamped to their ears, holding brown envelopes. Sean Burton was there dancing about waving his envelope in the air making a squeaky sound which didn't actually mean he'd passed or nothing 'cos he's proper flamboyant at the best of times. Kezia Marshall was sitting on a seat with her envelope resting on her bump looking at her result slip looking proper sad.

"'Ere, Shiraz, did you see Luther on your way here?" she shouted, and I shrugged and said no.

Coming in the door behind us were Chantalle Strong and Uma Brunton-Fletcher, stinking of ciggies, and in the corner was Nabila Chaalan being filmed by her dad opening her results and looking well pleased. By this point I was feeling seriously like I was going to have runnybum right there in my knickers.

"I'm Shiraz Bailey Wood," I said to Dora, the headmaster's secretary — as if she didn't flaming know — I saw more of Dora than I did of any of the teachers during Year Nine. She winked and got me my envelope. I stuck it under my arm and wandered off by myself outside to this little bench by the teachers' parking lot.

I could hardly breathe by this point. This is what it said:

CANDIDATE STATEMENT OF PROVISIONAL RESULTS
GENERAL CERTIFICATE OF SECONDARY EDUCATION

CENTER NUMBER: 64276
CENTER NAME: mayflower academy
CANDIDATE NUMBER: 2987
CANDIDATE NAME: wood, shiraz bailey
UNIQUE CANDIDATE IDENTIFIER: 6427568798768Q

TYPE	SUBJECT	RESULT
GCSE	English Lang.	A+
GCSE	English Lit.	A+
GCSE	Mathematics	C
GCSE	Religious Stu.	A
GCSE	History	A
GCSE	French	B
GCSE	Geography	B
GCSE	Applied Sci.	E
GCSE	Art	D

I stared at the paper for ages. I could NOT bloody believe it.

I got two A pluses!! And another two As! And some Bs and Cs! I got results like a proper bloody boffin would get! My heart was jumping about in my chest and I kept reading the name part again and again to double-check it weren't a mistake but it WEREN'T A MISTAKE! There was my name on the top and there ain't any other Shiraz Bailey Woods in the world ever! Go and stick my name in Google if you want proof! I'd passed a load of GCSEs! I PASSED ENGLISH AND MATH AND HISTORY AND RELIGION! I felt proper dizzy and sick and like I really needed the loo again. Then I stood up and sat down and stood up again and then I felt all floaty. I got my cell phone out to call my mum or someone. Then I put it back in my pocket again.

Just then a black 4×4 Jeep pulled into the parking lot with the windows down, playing some proper old skool R&B from the '90s. There was a dark-skinned lady wearing trendy thick-rimmed glasses in the driver's seat. Ms. Bracket! She got out and slammed the car door, spotted me, and gave me a wave.

"Well, good morning, Miss Wood," she said. "I was hoping I might see you!"

"All right, Ms. Bracket!" I said, but my voice was all crackly now like I was going to cry or something which was well shameful but I couldn't stop it.

"So, go on, then?" she said, nodding at the exam slip.

"I passed them!" I said. "I got two bloody A-pluses too! S'cuse my language, sorry! Look! I got loads of them . . ."

She took the sheet and looked at it and her face all lit up.

"My word, Shiraz Bailey Wood!" she said. "This is WONDER-FUL news. Totally. You absolutely deserve this! Well done!"

"Thanks very much!" I said and I was proper beginning to cry now, like a right loon. Ms. Bracket put her hand on my shoulder.

"Now, Shiraz, in my capacity as the new Head of English," she said, "I'm really hoping you'll be joining us in the brand-new Mayflower Sixth Form. I'm looking forward to teaching you. Actually, hang on a minute. Take one of these. They're just back from the printer."

Ms. Bracket reached inside her briefcase and pulled out a booklet that was titled "Mayflower Sixth Form — A Center of Excellence."

Just then Mr. Bamblebury, our headmaster, appeared looking all depressed and told Ms. Bracket he needed to talk to her about schedules.

I shoved my results in my hoodie pocket and walked slowly back to Mr. Yolk's where Mario had run out of both beef and chicken pot pies and the customers were staging some sort of revolt.

I got the rest of the teacups well white with no stains or anything. It took a lot of scrubbing though. As I say, it was a proper weird day.

TUESDAY 26TH AUGUST

The reason I didn't call no one yesterday when I got my results was 'cos to be honest I didn't want the hassle.

But I get home tonight to find Cava-Sue has organized a special dinner round at our house for the family and invited Nan and Wesley. Cava-Sue even went to the supermarket and got me one of them cakes where they use their computer to stick your face on the front which was proper sweet of her even if she had taken my old school photo from Year Eight where I've got my hair scraped back and a big spam forehead going on and a bit of a cross-eye and I look like a mental.

So I walk in the house and Nan and her mate Clement are in the living room drinking tea. Nan and Clement go everywhere together these days since their other mate Gill died proper sudden this year. I reckon they like seeing each other every day to make sure one of them can't go and cark it when the other one's not looking. Clement is a well funny old dude. He comes from the West Indies and he has this proper thoughtful way of saying everything like he knows a little bit about everything in the world. He always wears a hat. He's about eighty or something. He loves cakes. That's all I know about Clement really.

"So I hear we have a genius in our midst, young Shiraz!" Clement says when he sees me.

"Oh, not really," I say to him. "I dunno how I did it really. Proper fluke it was I reckon."

"Don't be daft!" says my Nan. "She's always been sharp as a tack this girl! 'Ere, Diane? Do you remember when she tried to donate our Murphy to the school's swap meet? Oh my life! I laughed and laughed."

"Nan, I was only seven," I said.

"Oh, but it was pure comedy," Nan said proper chuckling. "Your teacher said bring in stuff from home you're sick of and you don't want no more! So you tried to give 'em Murphy! You don't miss a trick, you!"

My mum walked in the living room then, carrying a teapot, still wearing her work uniform, laughing her head off.

"So I gets a call from the school, Clement," she says. "Saying 'ere Mrs. Wood your Shiraz in Primary Three has got your Murphy out of his Primary One class and she's sat him on a chair in the assembly hall with a price tag on his neck and he's doing his nut crying and had an accident in his trousers!! Oh, I shouldn't laugh but it were funny, bless 'em!"

"I weren't laughing," Murphy said proper grumpily 'cos he was trying to watch a *Regis and Kelly* rerun. Me and Murphy have both heard this story so many times now we could sing it like a song.

In the kitchen Cava-Sue and Lewis were sticking Iceland mini-sausages on sticks and pushing them in a melon to make a porcupine.

Next up my Wesley arrives and he's only gone and been to Kay in Ilford mall and got me a passing my exams pressie! It was a big gold heart-shaped locket on a chain with room for two photos.

"The woman in the shop says you gotta put me on one side and you on the other side and then when it's shut we'll always be kissing, innit," Wesley told me.

"Aw, isn't that smashing?" said my mum, looking at it proper jealously.

"Thanks, babe, you're a star," I said to Wesley.

I couldn't stop staring at it 'cos it was well big. Even bigger than Uma Brunton-Fletcher's clown pendant. Ginormous.

At that point Dad got back from work so we were all allowed to start eating. 'Cept we couldn't 'cos Cava-Sue wanted to make a speech, 'cos ever since she did that AS-Level in Theater Studies she can't do nothing without it turning into a big show.

"I just wanted to say on behalf of everyone," said Cava-Sue, clinking a glass with a spoon, "How proud of our Shiraz we all are that she's passed so many GCSEs! Shiz, I think you've got a really amazing future ahead of you. So here's to you! Cheers!"

Cava-Sue raised up her glass of Peach Lambrella wine.

"Cheers!" shouted everyone and we clinked our glasses together.

If we'd all just said goodnight then and gone our individual ways then we might have avoided the fight.

"So what's the plan now, Shiraz, is it next stop Downing Street?" said Clement, who was tucking into a piece of cake with my nose printed on it.

"Oh well, dunno really," I said to him, though I did know really. I was proper faking it.

"Yeah you do, Shiz," jumped in Cava-Sue. "You're going back to Sixth Form!"

"She's what?" said my mother. "No she ain't! She's got a job!"

Cava-Sue tutted well loudly. "Shiraz ain't got a proper job, Mum! She works at Mr. flaming Yolk!" she said, and she poked me in the arm well hard. "Shiz, have you not told Mother what you're doing?"

"Well I didn't know what I was doing!" I moaned.

"Well you do now," said Cava-Sue. "You're doing Sixth Form! You can't just stop now. You wanna get a proper education!"

Murphy and Wesley started to try to leave the room.

"Oh, bleeding wonderful!" said Mum, pointing at me. "Another one of my kids farting about after school instead of earning a living!"

Cava-Sue looked annoyed then.

"I was NOT farting about!" shouted Cava-Sue, "I took bloody AS-Levels in Theater Studies and General Studies. I passed them both too! I was in London when the results came so NO ONE THREW ME A PARTY!"

"Oh well, that may be, Cava-Sue!" shouted Mum, "But I thought you were doing them exams so you'd get an important job afterward and earn some cash! But you ain't got jack! Just floating about from one thing to the next! I'm still footing the bill!"

"Right! Come on," said Nan. "We've all had a drink! Let's just pipe down!"

We'd only had bleeding half a bottle of Peach Lambrella between nine of us!

"Me and Lewis are going traveling!" shouted Cava-Sue, pointing at Lewis, who was trying to hide behind the sausage porcupine. "That's why we're not starting our careers yet! And to be quite frank, Mother, it ain't all about getting a proper flashy job anyway. What about education just for education's sake!? What about just bettering your brain!?"

Mum looked well hacked off now.

"Well, my brain is fine thank you and I didn't do any of these AS level thingies!" shouted my mum, "I got myself a job the very second I could. I wasn't even sixteen! I was fifteen! Clive, the manager at Edmund Bosworth Bookies — God rest his mortal soul — had to pay me out of the petty cash float 'cos I was too young to legally work! But I was on the doorstep at 8AM every day and I went there with PRIDE."

"Oh really, Mother?" sighed Cava-Sue proper snarky like. "Do tell me that again. I've only heard it EIGHT MILLION NINE HUNDRED AND TWELVE TIMES since I was born."

Suddenly, I had to say what was burning up in my head, 'cos it was dying to get out.

"LOOK, EVERYONE! SHUT UP A MINUTE," I shouted. Everyone shut up and looked at me. "I WANNA GO BACK TO SIXTH FORM, RIGHT! I WANNA DO SOME A-LEVELS!"

No one said anything. They all stared at me with their gobs open. Mum just pursed her lips. My dad gave me a wink. I could see him trying not to smile.

When I got home from Mr. Yolk the next day I went in my room and Dad was fitting together a desk in the corner. It's only a little one from Target with a fold-up chair, but it's a proper place for me to study.

Ha! "A proper place for me to study."

Oh my days, listen to me, I am such a flaming boffin.

SEPTEMBER

The Ilford Bugle

TIME FOR A FRESH START, SAYS
"SUPERCHAV ACADEMY" HEAD
— reporter Mark E. Taylor

A brand new Sixth Form "center of excellence" and banner GCSE results spell a fresh start for Mayflower Academy, claims optimistic headmaster Siegmund Bamblebury.

Mayflower Academy — nicknamed "Superchav Academy" by the national press following a catalogue of antisocial behavior issues — has recently received a multi-million-pound cash-boost from central government. The funds have been plowed into renovating and extending the school, as well as employing new teaching staff and restocking the library.

"I want to draw a line through the old days. It's time the media stopped harking back to the negative," said Mr. Bamblebury, making reference to the widescale drug use, joy-riding, bullying, and low exam grades which led to a 2004 Ofsted inspection to term the establishment "The worst school in Britain."

"It's important to look ahead, not backward," said Mr. Bamblebury. "The past two years have seen massive improvements."

When asked about last December's Mayflower Winter Festival, which resulted in the assembly hall being destroyed by fire, Mr. Bamblebury put the phone down and curtailed the interview.

TUESDAY 2ND SEPTEMBER

I wandered over to Carrie's tonight 'cos Carrie's mum Maria was having a party for Carrie passing her GCSEs. Carrie didn't do quite as well as me, but she still got three A's, which is well good 'cos she didn't do nothing to prepare as far as I could tell.

Maria wanted to celebrate last week but then Carrie's dad Barney got this big old contract fitting Jacuzzis all over Chigwell. This geezer called Malik who works in the city had got a ginormous cash bonus through so he'd bought EVERY SINGLE MEMBER OF HIS FAMILY a Jacuzzi for their garden. Barney was over the moon. He's not been home for days except to sleep. "You gotta make hay when the sun shines!" That's what Barney Draper always says. "I ain't gonna keep my little girl in daft shoes and lip gloss sitting about on my 'arris contemplating my navel!" he says.

I like Carrie's dad a lot, he's got all that cash but he ain't posh or nothing. I mean, he might wear expensive shirts and flash his wallet a bit when he goes down to the dog races at Walthamstow but he ain't up himself. I like Carrie's mum, too. She's a little bit posh, mind. "Posher than she ought to be!" my mother always says.

My mother's got beef with Maria 'cos Maria was once a barmaid at the Goodmayes Social and always used to be proper brassic. Then all of a sudden she's married to this plumber called Barney and Barney's started up his own little business and they ain't living in Dovehill Close no more, they're living in Swansbrook Drive in a duplex and driving a car with a sunroof and instead of collecting one Victorian figurine at a time out of *Star* magazine, Maria's got enough cash to buy the whole bloody lot in one go AND put them in their own revolving display cabinet with spotlights THEN place the cabinet beside a tropical fish tank. By the time Maria and Barney were building their own country-style mansion house on the other side of Goodmayes and calling it Draperville and putting up electric gates and doing their special charity Christmas light display, well my mother was so riled she couldn't say Maria's name without pulling a face like you would if you took a slurp out of a milk carton then realized the milk had turned to liquid stilton cheese.

So I'm sitting in the dining room at Draperville tonight and me and Carrie are eating massive pieces of triple chocolate truffle cake that Maria got made by this cake-maker she knows in Epping Forest who makes cakes for celebrities — like folk in *EastEnders* — for birthdays and all that. She once made the Queen Vic totally out of nougat, sponge, icing sugar, and gumdrops. It was on the front of the *Ilford Bugle*. Anyway, Carrie's cake was in the shape of an open book to symbolize all the hard study Carrie had put into passing her GCSEs which sort of made me laugh 'cos what would have REALLY symbolized Carrie passing her GCSEs would be a cake with marzipan figurines of Carrie snoring on her bed with *Butterz to Babe in Thirty Days* over her face while I read *Jane Eyre* beside her shouting, "Carrie! Wake up, you lazy cow!"

"Well, I'd just like to raise a toast to my daughter," Maria was saying. "I'm so proud of what you've done, love. And so proud that you're carrying on at school to get some A-Levels!"

"'Ere, and not only A-Levels," butted in Barney all proud like.

"Then off to university to do a business studies degree or something! Before you know it you could be running the whole bloody company! Give your old dad some time off with his newspaper!"

Maria and Barney both looked quite choked up then.

"Yeah," Carrie said, then she gave them both a kiss and we all raised our glasses of Moet and Chambum champagne, which is this well posh stuff that Barney always gets out on special occasions which is well dear but always makes my breath taste like sick.

"Cheers everybody." Maria smiled, showing her sparkly white teeth that she's just had Da Vinci veneers put on.

"Up yer bums!" shouted Barney, raising his glass.

Me and Carrie went upstairs afterward and we lay on her bed and watched *Yo Momma!* on MTV and Carrie pulled out my "straggler" eyebrows and pushed back my cuticles with a hard stick. And let's just say she weren't as lively as I'd be if Barney Draper had just said I could have his whole bloody company. Maybe she's on her period.

THURSDAY 4TH SEPTEMBER

Cava-Sue and Lewis have changed their travel plans. They were going to fly to Vietnam on December 1st then stay there for the magical festival of Moonyflunkcock (I reckon that's what she said, I was earwigging on her cell phone call). Then they're moving on to Thailand afterward to check out some waterfalls and temples. Cava-Sue says she needs to leave Britain so she can really "challenge her Western world ways of perception."

After Thailand they're going to Australia to meet their mate Pixie 'cos apparently the pubs there are great.

What's messed all this up is that Lewis's mother, Vera, has told them she won't be able to give them a loan as planned 'cos the profits in her pub ain't up to much at the moment. Cava-Sue has been ringing around for a credit card but no one wants to give her one. Cava-Sue says they'll have to put back their departure date to February now.

My mother says that'll give Cava-Sue and Lewis time to "travel" to the Ilford job center and "check out the magical festival of cold hard work." We all laughed for ages when she said that except for Cava-Sue, who burst into tears.

FRIDAY 5TH SEPTEMBER

I was walking home from work tonight down Thundersley Road well buzzing 'cos after tomorrow I'll only be working at Mr. Yolk on Saturdays. Believe me, eight hours a week is too long to spend with Mario. Especially when you're the bloody negotiator between him and the Great British public who are trying to change bits of his set breakfasts. "No, Shirelle!" he moans at me. "Tell them they NO have mushrooms instead of beans! Set Breakfast C come with beans! I no their slave! They eat what Mr. Yolk serve! Set Breakfast C is perfect combination of item. I not mess about with it!!"

So anyway, I'm nearly home tonight and I see Clinton Brunton-Fletcher with his red hair shaved coming toward me on the pavement on a BMX that's well too small for him like it must be jacked off some young kid. He's not really looking where he's going, then he spots me and goes "Shizz" and I'm like, "All right, Clint." And then he blasts off down the road and next I hear Uma's voice screaming after him, "Cliiiiiiiinton! You ain't leaving me in here with all that stuff!" But there was no point as he was well gone.

I looked down the road and Uma was standing in her front garden which is looking even more dodgy than ever these days 'cos it now actually has a fridge and sofa in it and the hedge has been burned down.

"Y'all right, Shizza," Uma shouted to me.

"Y'all right, Uma." I shouted back. I didn't want to walk down and chat with her but I knew if I didn't it would get all blown up into some big diss, so I went up and thought I'd keep it well brief. "What you up to?" I said.

"Aw. Nothing. Just staying in with Zeus and watching telly," she said. Just then Uma's Staffy, Zeus, came running out of the house being all big and scary. He's a big brindle Staffy with a studded collar.

Uma is actually pretty sometimes when you look at her and forget who she is. She is dead tall with big brown eyes and has sort of prominent teeth that are always white and she's skinny with long legs and a little waist. She wears quite hoochie clothes though. Skin-tight leggings and crop tops and short mini-skirts. And she goes mental if she thinks someone is disrespecting her which is pretty much always 'cos she is well paranoid. I've known Uma since I was in preschool. My mum don't like Uma at all. When Uma's stepdad got sent to jail for dealing shed loads of weed last January my mum was overjoyed 'cos she thought the Brunton-Fletchers would get an ASBO and be moved off somewhere else in Essex. "Good riddance to bad rubbish!" Mum said. "They've been spoiling this road since the second they landed here."

What actually happened was Rose, Uma's mum, moved up to Durham temporarily to be nearer the jail and took the youngest kids with her and now Uma and Clinton live by themselves with Zeus. People get all uptight about Zeus but I know for a fact he ain't no devil dog and he sleeps in Uma's bed every night with her arms wrapped around him like a bloody hot water bottle. He's like the only family she's got left. Well, aside from Clinton, but he don't really count.

"Want a joint?" said Uma.

"Nah, I promised Mum I'd make my dad's tea," I said, which was a lie. I can't stand the smell of weed, let alone bloody smoke any.

"Ah, well, never mind, I'm giving up myself." She shrugged. "See you on Monday though, innit?"

"Errrrm, what we doing on Monday?" I said.

"I'm starting in Sixth Form," she said.

I tried my very very best to stop my face saying, "UMA, HOW THE BLOODY HELL HAVE YOU GOT INTO SIXTH FORM?" — 'cos like I say, Uma is proper paranoid anyway and smoking skunk ain't doing her no favors.

BUT, HONESTLY, HOW???? HOW!?

MONDAY 8TH SEPTEMBER

1AM — OMG I start Sixth Form today.

3AM — I'm still awake. Can't sleep at all.

5AM — Aaaaagh! I'm wide awake again and I can't bloody get back to sleep as I am bricking it about school. You know something? I don't think I quite thought this whole thing through. I reckon I just got all swept away with Ms. Bracket and her "master of your own destiny" speech 'cos Ms. Bracket is like Yoda or something. She is well crafty at fooling kids into thinking they are good when they think they ain't worth nothing and that's what she did to me. She's a proper headbend that woman is.

Maybe my mother is right. At least Mr. Yolk's was a job and it was bringing in money and I should have been proud of the fact I was supporting myself with no handouts from no one. Maybe my mother is right. Maybe I'll be laughing on the other side of my face when I'm back next week crying to Mr. Yolk wanting all my hours back and he's given them to some Polish woman who works twice as hard for half as much. I won't feel so bleeding clever then my mother says.

5:25AM — I think I am having what Dr. Oz on *Oprah* would call an "anxiety attack" as I'm proper panicking now and I don't even know what to wear today and I don't know what to take with me and I don't even know what bloody subjects to do when I get there. Cava-Sue said yesterday I should put on something comfortable and take a pen with me and just "enjoy the experience." Cava-Sue says I've got to stop being so bleeding theatrical.

Me, theatrical? HA HA HA. She was only at college in Ilford half a week and she went all emo and began prancing about in a stripey sweater and a hat with a pom pom and scarf looking like him off of *Where's Waldo*?

I don't wanna change if I go to Sixth Form. I like being me.

7:30AM — Have just called Carrie for wardrobe advice. Carrie reckons the dress code today is "smart-casual" or "smart-caj" as she is calling it. Carrie says there is a section on smart-caj in the "Dress to Impress" chapter of her *Butterz to Babe* book. Carrie says that Tabitha Tennant says that smart-caj means "businesslike with a chilled-out twist, possibly with a nod toward sportswear."

EH? What does that mean? That newscaster blouse Mum got me for Aunty Glo's silver wedding anniversary party with some track pants? My mother's betting-shop jacket with my Von Dutch cap and carrying along a Ping-Pong paddle?

8AM — Right. This is what I'm wearing: My best jeans from TopShop. My pink T-shirt with the white swirls on it from Wet Seal. My pink Ellesse trainers, and my white McKenzie hoodie. I'm wearing my hair loose and back in a gold metal headband and my big gold hoops. That's final. I ain't changing again. End of.

8:15AM — Oh and my gold locket that Wesley bought me of course with the pictures of us in it from when we went to see DJ Tim Westwood. I gotta wear it 'cos Wesley's giving me a lift to school and he gets the hump a little bit if I don't 'cos it cost a proper bomb and it was money he could have spent on rims. Gotta go.

TUESDAY 9TH SEPTEMBER

OH MY DAYS. Yesterday was proper hectic. I'm going to try and write it all down as this will certainly be a well important chapter in the life of Shiraz Bailey Wood when I give my diaries over to the person who writes my autobiography.

So we got to Mayflower School in the morning and we turfed out Murphy from the backseat for his first day in Year Ten then Wesley held my hand for a bit and he was all like, "Good luck, Shizza, you'll be fine. Don't worry, innit."

But to be quite honest Wesley looked more worried than me. 'Specially when he saw all these boys going into the new Sixth Form center all bustin' their proper best clothes like they were going to a shubz not to school at all.

So Wesley says to me, "Shiraz? Do you, like, know all of these Sixth Form boys and that, innit?"

And I said like, "Nah. Not really," 'cos I hardly reconized any faces. For the first time I suddenly realized that Mayflower Sixth Form weren't just going to be Mayflower School kids that I knew. It was going to be kids coming from all other schools too — like Regis Hill Boys Academy and Walthamstow Grange and Thomas Duke in Leytonstone.

I felt really sick again then 'cos I think I'd been fooling myself that me and Carrie were going to stride in there and it was going to be like our turf and all people we knew. Now I saw that we were going to be swamped with all these totally new folks and we were going to be new girls too.

So I kiss Wesley goodbye and I walk into the new Sixth Form Center and there's this big white room with sofas and beanbags in it that looks like somewhere to hang out between classes and there's all these kids just standing about reading the Center of Excellence handbook and there's loads of Year Nines and Year Tens all outside pushing their faces up against the window and staring in at us like we were fish in a tank while teachers kept shouting at them to move away.

There was a little kitchen in the corner with a tea kettle and a microwave, and a TV at the far side of the room which was already turned on and this boy with floppy brown hair, baggy jeans, and proper strong cheekbones was watching *Fast-Track Family Feud* presented by Reuben Smart. The cheekbone lad was laughing well loud at the folks who go on that show. "Look at this lot, Saf!" he was saying to his mate who was this well choong black kid sitting beside him sending a text, wearing those limited-edition Nikes they just got in Niketown that every boy is going on about. "Where do they find these nutters?!" he was saying, pointing at the telly. I moved away from the TV dead quick and said nothing.

Finally, after what seemed like about eighteen hours standing on my own feeling like I had a big flashing silver spangly arrow hovering above my head saying **BILLY NO MATES,** the door opens and Carrie, Luther Dinsdale, and Nabila Chaalan walk in. Then not long behind is Sean Burton and Sonia Cathcart all looking very "smart-caj." Even Nabila had a bit of mascara and jewelry on with her hijab which she don't normally. Carrie, whose fake tan was looking very "Month in Trinidad," was wearing a black skirt and a black top with long sleeves and sort of floaty

41

cuffs and long brown boots I ain't never seen before and looking well WAGish.

All of us from Mayflower were like "Wooo-hoo!" when we met up. Even me and Sonia Cathcart were pleased to see each other which is sort of weird 'cos I ain't never really been that great mates with Sonia ever since Year Eight when her family went all born-again Christian and she once told me that 'cos I weren't confirmed a Christian and didn't eat and drink the body of Christ on Sunday then I was going to be pretty much shafted once the day of reckoning came 'cos there would be a great storm and she'd be up in heaven and I'd be left down here with THE BEAST.

So I says to her, "well FAIR PLAY, Sonia, 'cos I'd rather be left down here with Satan nibbling my 'arris than up in heaven with your father and his bloody tambourine and his megaphone that he uses to jar everyone's head about Jesus Christ outside Food Lion every Saturday and by the way, Sonia, my mother reckons your father ain't that flipping holy 'cos he's always in her betting shop and she reckons he ain't been touched by Jesus he's just having some sort of mental episode and he needs his head looked at by Dr. Gupta!"

Well, it all went off then and I wasn't allowed back to Religious Studies until I apologized to Sonia in a letter. But as I say that was a long time ago back in Year Eight and it's all good now. It's just I wouldn't exactly call Sonia my best friend or nothing. Not Nabila Chaalan neither. But it was funny 'cos yesterday as me, Sean, Nabila, and everyone looked about the Sixth Form we realized that this little gang were pretty much all we'd got.

Then the door opens and Uma Brunton-Fletcher walks in. She's wearing black leggings and a denim mini and a black hoodie, and thick gold hoops with her gold clown pendant over the top. Her hair was tied up in a scrunchie in an "Ilford Face Lift," as my mother calls it. Everybody who knew her tried not to look shocked to see her but they did anyhow.

"All right," she said to us all then she pretended to look at her phone, but the moment she went to the loo Sonia goes in a loud whisper, "WHAT IS UMA BRUNTON-FLETCHER DOING HERE!?" Then Carrie says that her mum says that she knows someone who works for the council and they reckon that Mayflower are letting some kids in to study who you'd never imagine doing further education so Mayflower can qualify for their government funding and look good in all the newspapers "'cos they're giving a chance to the pikeys."

I felt sick again then 'cos I started thinking that Carrie's mum's friend was meaning folk like me too.

Most of the rest of the day I spent running about signing up for my courses. I've signed up for AS-Level English Literature, History, Film Studies, and Critical Thinking. It all looks well hard. I saw Ms. Bracket and she says I've picked "a good mix of arts subjects which is an area I've shown great aptitude for and should find a wonderful challenge." I love the way she takes something proper scary and makes it sound like a big exciting game. Carrie is doing English Lit and Film Studies too so at least I'll have someone to sit with now and again.

I still don't know if I'm doing the right thing here. I still don't know if I'm a Sixth Former sort of person. Some of these new lot seem right up themselves. Like yesterday, I was standing in line to sign up for Critical Thinking and this boy was standing one in front of me making a right old fuss. (I figured out later it was the same lad who was laughing at *Fast-Track Family Feud.*)

So anyways, he's at the desk and I'm behind waiting and I'm waiting and waiting and waiting 'cos he's taking all day to sign up 'cos he's asking all about the course in tiny detail and Mr. Stockford is saying, "Joshua! All will be explained at the first lesson!" and this Joshua lad with the cheekbones is going, "But I need to know now! Why would I officially sign up for a subject without knowing the full extent of the syllabus!" which I sort of agreed with but I wouldn't have put it so posh, I'd have said "'Ere, bruv, I ain't signing nothing now. What am I, some sort of clown?!"

Anyways, after about another ten minutes of bickering Mr. Stockford says, "OK! OK! Joshua Fallow, we will keep a provisional place in the course open for you! Come to the induction lesson and you can sign the papers when you feel certain."

With that I give a huge sigh of relief and go 'Halle-bloody-lujah!" and this Joshua turns round and stares at me. Then he looks me right up and down like I'm a bloody mannequin in Top-Shop and he's checking out the new season's autumn/winter fashion.

"Who are you then? Are you doing Critical Thinking too?" he goes.

He had swimming-pool-blue eyes and clear, tanned skin and nice lips.

"I'm Shiraz Bailey Wood," I said proper back in his face.

"Shiraz Bailey Wood?" Joshua was cocking his head to the side like our Penny does when she's angling for a bit of your Kit Kat. "Shiraz?" he repeated. "As in the wine?

"Yeah," I said.

"And Bailey?" he said. I flared my nostrils at him.

"Like as in the Irish cream liqueur," I said looking him right in the eye like I had no fear.

"Shiraz Bailey Wood," he said again.

"Yeah," I said.

"I'm Joshua Ezra Fallow," he said.

"All right, Joshua," I said, pulling my best "Whatever, bruv" face.

"Wowzers! That's a big locket," he said, nodding at Wesley's pressie.

"Yeah, thanks very much," I said, then I pushed past him and went to register. He's one of them blokes who's good-looking but knows it so he's a bit up himself. Like I said, I can't stand boys like that.

9:15PM — Just been speaking to Cava-Sue and she says she is well chuffed for me signing up for all these courses. Cava-Sue says don't WHATEVER I do tell mother about doing Film Studies 'cos she will say it's just lying about on your arse eating gummies and it totally isn't.

9:30PM — Yeah bare jokes, Cava-Sue! You're kidding, right? Next thing you'll be saying for English Lit AS-Level I actually have to read ALL of those books on Ms. Bracket's list, including Shakespeare's *King Lear* and *Henry IV* Part One! Ha ha ha ha!

THURSDAY 11TH SEPTEMBER

Cava-Sue and Lewis have got new jobs. They're working at Sunshine Sandwiches at Ilford. There's stacks of jobs going there right now 'cos everyone got fired last week after an investigation by Head Office discovered people giving out free ketchup packets and drink refills to their mates. Cava-Sue and Lewis have to wear salmon-pink trousers and burgundy T-shirts and green baseball hats that say "LET ME MAKE YOU A SUNSHINE SANDWICH!" Cava-Sue says it will do for a few months. Cava-Sue says it'll be worth it when she's in Northern Thailand "communing" with the long-necked women of Mae Hong Son.

Sometimes I wonder if Cava-Sue regrets not carrying on after AS-Level and doing A2-Level. She don't ever say. She only talks about traveling now. Traveling to weird places where you need ten injections in your jacksie before you set off and special knickers just to stop bum-invading ants scampering up your passages and nibbling your kidneys. Rather her than me.

The thing I find freaky is that our Cava-Sue never even mentioned traveling before she started seeing Lewis. Traveling was his big dream, NOT hers at all. That freaks me out about boyfriends. It seems that when you're with them for a while, you start losing track of what you actually want. They bend your bloody head.

FRIDAY 12TH SEPTEMBER

Oh thank God it is Friday. I am KNACKERED. I've spent the whole week at Mayflower having my first AS lessons, or to be more exact, sitting on a chair in a circle playing "getting to know you" games with folk from Regis Hill, Walthamstow Grange and other schools. "Everyone pick a partner!" shouted Ms. Bracket in the first AS English course. "Spend five minutes telling each other your interests! Then report back to the group!"

So, it turns out I don't have any interests. Not real ones anyway.

I mean, what do I ever bloody do? Go shopping? (Not even shopping, just "looking" 'cos I am brassic). See Wesley? Watch *EastEnders*? Mess about on MySpace? Apparently these DON'T count. Not when there's a girl in my Sixth Form called Tonita who goes to Lea Valley Ice Rink three times a week and wants to compete in London 2012. Not when there's a Sikh boy called Manpreet who once was on *Countdown* and won £1,000!! Saying that, he's a proper weirdo who's also made a complete Wembley Stadium out of matchsticks so I'm not that jealous.

That Joshua Fallow lad is a PROPER NUISANCE. Joshua Fallow reckons that I can't have "Seeing My Nan" as an interest. Or "Singing" neither, if it's only when I'm in the shower. Joshua Fallow reckons they don't count. Who died and made him king?! Joshua Fallow reckons I should have "Weight lifting" down as one of my hobbies 'cos I must have been training my neck muscles for months to cart around my gold hoops and my locket at the same time.

I told Joshua Fallow his "interest" should be sitting on the mantelpiece frightening small kids away from the fire, 'cos his face looks like a cat's fangita. Joshua laughed for ages when I said that. He is ANNOYING.

SUNDAY 14TH SEPTEMBER

Today Nan came over and cooked us Sunday dinner. I love it when Nan cooks dinner 'cos she makes everything, even stuff like broccoli, taste amazing and everything is hot at the same time and the chicken is crispy on the outside and white and soft in the middle and the gravy just tastes like the best thing in the world ever 'cos she makes it in a well-complicated way with all the stuff from the chicken pan and this brown floury powder. She doesn't just pour water into a mix like Mum. If I had to die tomorrow and I was allowed one last meal I would ask for some of Nan's roast potatoes and her gravy. Straight up, I would.

Mum gets a bit narked if I say stuff like this though, so I have to make a big point of saying I like her waffles, SpaghettiO's, and sausage dinners too. Wesley came round for Sunday dinner today 'cos his mum's in Blackpool at a Motown Tribute Festival this weekend so he was on his own and was planning to have Chef Boyardee. Wesley loves my nan's roast potatoes. In fact Wesley loves Nan too and he even calls her Nan which she really likes. Wesley must have been extra hungry today 'cos he ate all of his dinner like one of them gorillas out of *Planet of the Apes*. I wish he would eat more like a human and try not to get gravy all over his face.

After the food, Wesley tried to get me to come out with him for a drive then go back to his house for a bit seeing as his mum's not back till tomorrow and we could have some "privacy." I knew what he was getting at so I said no I needed to read *King Lear.* Wesley looked a bit like he might get the hump, then he chilled out and said no bother.

Wesley went over to his mate Bezzie Kelleher's house instead. Bezzie used to go out with Carrie about a year and half ago, but they split up on account of his being a proper bell-end. Wesley says Bezzie's been laying some more tracks down and wonders whether Wesley fancies spitting some lyrics. Bezzie wants to get their "rhyme syndicate" the G-Mayes Detonators back together and do some collaborations with some of the other crews they know like the Crowley Park Brapboys and the Rinse and Go Fraternity. I said, "Yeah, that sounds like a good idea. Bezzie is proper talented," and made a face like I totally meant it.

I started reading *King Lear.* As far as I can see it's about this old geezer who is a king who feels knackered so reckons he might pack in his job, so right away all his daughters start being well shady trying to work out ways to nick all his money. It's a bit like that time old Bob down at number 47 died sudden in the night and by about 11AM his garden was full of all his sons proper fighting over his jar of loose coins and his gold sovereign ring and his Status Quo records.

Money does weird things to folks. That's one good thing about having none.

MONDAY 15TH SEPTEMBER

Classes are well hard in Sixth Form. We're reading *King Lear* in English and Ms. Bracket isn't hanging back waiting for us to pick it up slowly, she's making us gallop through it, reading it out and acting bits and firing us loads of questions. Carrie is looking well cheesed off. She says she's not feeling it at all. Manpreet says he read *King Lear* twice when he was eleven. WHAT A FREAK.

I can't believe Uma is still here. She sat beside me and Carrie in English today and she remembered her book and everything even if she did look proper baffled all the way through the lesson. Sonia Cathcart said to me in study hall that Uma is only doing, like, one AS-Level and it's NOT FAIR 'cos Uma's only there 'cos she's "One of Ms. Bracket's little charity projects."

I felt my face go hot then and I said to Sonia Cathcart she should go say that to Uma's face if she's such a rudegirl and so Sonia shut up. I dunno why I started sticking up for Uma, I just did. I reckon it's 'cos there's some folk in Sixth Form who think they're well better than others and I ain't into that at all. You've got to keep it real.

That Joshua Fallow hadn't read any of *King Lear* 'cos he said he had to help his mum out selling her paintings on Saturday at her art stall at Spitalfields Market. Not only does Joshua have proper interests, HIS MOTHER DOES TOO.

"Well you had all Sunday, Joshua!" Ms. Bracket said sternly.

"Yes, and I planned to read it," Joshua said. "But then I went out for brunch with my parents to Applebees in Leytonstone and when I got back my dad started watching his DVD boxset of *The Sopranos* Season 4 which, interestingly enough, we both agreed contained a lot of striking Shakespearian parallels, y'know, with it focusing on an aging leader and his children jostling for power."

Ms. Bracket smiled when he said that and let him off. Joshua Fallow gets off with stuff a lot 'cos he's got the gift of gab. And he's properly good-looking. Not just "oh yeah he's sort of buff" good-looking but in an "oh my days dat boy is bare choong" sort of good-looking. Not that I think that but other girls do.

11PM — And what is BRUNCH???

TUESDAY 16TH SEPTEMBER

One of the reasons I feel sorry for Uma is that despite the fact she's trying proper hard to be like a normal Sixth Former, and despite the fact she's totally trying not to drop-kick Sonia Cathcart across the common room then finish her off with a karate chop when Sonia makes those little comments about how hard FOUR AS-LEVELS are if you have to do four of them WHICH SONIA DOES BY THE WAY . . . none of this matters. 'Cos just as folks are beginning to chill out a bit and forget that Uma is a Brunton-Fletcher then BLOODY CLINTON BRUNTON-FLETCHER starts turning up around the school gates on his bloody tiny BMX, selling weed to folk as young as Year Ten. KNOBHEAD.

"Can't you tell him to stop?" Sonia Cathcart said proper loudly to Uma today in study hall. Oh my days I hope Sonia Cathcart's god is looking down on her 'cos she is going to get one good old proper ass-whooping on the day Uma gets kicked out and has nothing to lose. Uma just opened her *King Lear* and pretended to read. "He ain't nothing to do with me," she said under her breath narkily.

FRIDAY 19TH SEPTEMBER

Clinton was up at the school again today. Hanging about looking well wide. I got Wesley to be a double agent tonight and ask our Murphy about whether he is buying any weed off Clinton 'cos if he is I'm going to be seriously narked 'cos I don't want him turning out like all those lads did when I was in Year Ten who got into smoking skunk and before you know it they're just sitting in the park smoking all the time and that's all they do, smoke smoke smoke and they end up like Cotch and Eric who Carrie once made us double-date and who act like they got some sort of brain damage. Or they end up like Luther who smoked some skunk so strong that he got Kezia Marshall pregnant and don't even remember doing it.

Wesley says that Murphy says that he ain't buying any weed off Clinton. Wesley says that one of Murphy's mates Delano is though. Murphy says that Delano's eighteen-year-old brother Janelle has already found out and is proper raging. Murphy says that Janelle rolls with some proper hoods and he's coming up to the school gates to kill Clinton.

I said to Wesley, "What does he mean *kill* Clinton?" and Wesley says he didn't ask 'cos he was trying to play it cool like James Bond and not ask too much. I feel sorry for Mr. Bamblebury, our headmaster. He was just on a news report showing off about Mayflower's "Bright new start" too.

WEDNESDAY 24TH SEPTEMBER

I'm quite enjoying History, but I don't go about telling folks. The only reason my mother is off my back right now about doing A-Levels is 'cos I always make a proper painful face when I mention school as if every day is like having your skin peeled off and rolled in toilet cleaner. If I hate it she'll keep making me go.

Today we were learning about Martin Luther who was this bloke in the 14th century who started the Protestant faith by writing this notice to the pope saying something like, "Oi Bruv, you are bare jokes mate. This Catholic faith malarkey is a right old ripoff." Then he hammers it up on a door and before you know it all sorts of beef has kicked off and there's this totally rival crew to the Catholics started up called the Protestants. I like History 'cos it proves you can do one little thing and the world can change forever. A bit like when Tabitha Tennant invented cupid-bow lips.

FRIDAY 26TH SEPTEMBER

11PM — I can't bloody believe what happened today. CAN'T BELIEVE IT. Right, so today me and Carrie and Sean and Joshua and Saf are all sitting in the Audio Visual room in the dark watching this film called *Secrets and Lies* for Film Studies which sounds like a right old doss but believe me it ain't 'cos you have to concentrate proper hard and try to work out how the filmmaker is "creating tension" and "building characters" which is NOTHING LIKE going to the AMC Loews where everyone chucks popcorn and farts and talks on their phones the whole way through.

So we're all in the dark and it's totally quiet aside from Carrie snoring and suddenly there is this well loud BANG outside. Like, BAAAAAAANG! Like a car backfiring proper loudly. Then seconds later loads of screaming and shouting. Then doors slamming and loads of noise in the halls and thundering feet and yelling and shrieking. So we all stand up and run to the window and look down onto the path up to the school gate and suddenly there's loads of Year Ten and Year Eleven kids outside all waving their arms and looking frightened and sickened and excited all at once like something proper amazing had just happened.

So I open the window and shout down to Tariq who is one of Murphy's friends, "Tariq, what's happened?"

And he shouts "Clinton Brunton-Fletcher has been shot! Someone has shot him, man! Brap Brap Braaaaaap!" And Tariq is waving his hands in the air giving gun signs looking sort of happy but sort of disgusted at the same time.

So I said, "What do you mean? Where's Clinton?"

Tariq said, "Dunno man, he's gone! Whoever shot him is well gone too!"

I backed away from the window, suddenly feeling well cold and sick, and by that point the bell was ringing and outside turned into total bloody chaos 'cos suddenly there was like a thousand kids all flocking around the main gate and everyone telling everyone else the tale that Clinton had been shot and Uma was in the center of it trying to talk on her cell phone looking proper upset. And then the police arrived blaring their sirens and then even more police arrived and then some news reporters arrived and then loads of parents arrived and then loads of passersby started loitering and everyone was shouting at each other and Mrs. Radowitz and Ms. Bracket were trying to push the kids back indoors. And by this point people were saying that they'd DEFINITELY seen the car and they'd definitely seen Clinton covered in blood and it weren't a small gun, no it was a big gun, in fact it was one of them proper gangster MAC-10 submachine guns and the gunman were on a moped, no in a Audi, no in a Benz Jeep. And there was four of them. No, five. Five gunmen in ski masks doing a drive-by shooting! Except one gunman took off his ski mask and a Year Seven lad saw it was DEFINITELY JANELLE.

This was all crap. No one had really *seen* anything, in fact the only people who'd seen anything at all was two Year Nine kids, Olivier and Mikey, and they were now saying that they saw Clinton on his BMX, then they just heard a bang, which was maybe just a car backfiring and then Clinton shouting out then pedaling away. But by this point that story seemed pretty BORING and everyone wanted to believe the gun story more and everyone wanted to be part of the drama, except Uma who now seemed to have disappeared, and there were girls crying and boys giving it the big one saying Clinton deserved to get merked and everyone was talking about gangs and guns and by this point Sky News had arrived on the scene and my mother called my cell and said that Mayflower was live on the telly on one of their big flashing News Flash bulletins that said, "SHOOTING AT SUPERCHAV ACADEMY."

Mum said I had to come home straightaway and I shouted, "Mum, I don't even think there's been a shooting!" and Mum shouted, "Well there's been something going on! It's all over the news! I'm watching your bloody school now! There's a police helicopter circling the school! Get yourself home RIGHT NOW!" So I says to her, "Mum I don't think that is a police helicopter I think that's maybe the Sky News helicopter filming the pictures that you're watching." Then she told me to stop being so bloody clever and get home before I got my head blown off.

I didn't go home. Me and Carrie hung about around the film crews for a while listening to news reporters do their reports. Loads of kids were trying to get into the camera shots and people who knew NOTHING about Mayflower School were suddenly turning up being a world flipping authority on the place which was making me proper angry. I was listening to this one guy wearing a suit and tie holding a microphone and he was going live on BBC and he was obviously just making up crap as he went along going something like . . .

"Well, Julia! Here I am, outside Mayflower Academy! Now, this is a school that has been DOGGED BY CONTROVERSY for a long time and it had seemed recently as though there had been some VAGUE IMPROVEMENTS, but now it's more of the same: weapons, gangs, violence, drug-dealing, and antisocial behavior! What a sad example of the youth of today this school is! I mean, to set the scene, this was the school that was once called the WORST SCHOOL IN BRITAIN providing some of the

lowest standards in education in the country. In turn it gained a nick-
name in media circles as "Superchav Academy" — chav being a term for
the very underclass, FERAL, out of control children we see all too often in
Britain today. Well the nickname CERTAINLY FITS TODAY, Julia, be-
cause here I am on the scene of what is looking to be a drive-by-shooting
incident! More news as we get it, this is me, Max Blackford, reporting for
BBC news, now back to the studio . . ."

This made me really really mad. Max Blackford didn't mention
that this maybe weren't even a shooting. Or if it was it HAD
NOTHING TO DO WITH MAYFLOWER KIDS, it was caused by
somebody who left years ago. Max didn't say there were lots of
really good kids at Mayflower. Or mention Tonita's ice-skating or
Manpreet's *Countdown* prize or the time Year Eight made that
Diplodocus out of egg cartons to give to the children's hospital
or the lad in Year Ten who got scouted for West Ham youth soccer squad last week! Or the fact that loads of kids at Mayflower
got proper GCSEs this year or the fact that we WEREN'T ALL
BLOODY CHAVS WHO WERE INTO SHOOTING EACH
OTHER, RIGHT????

So when Max bloody Bratford asked me and Carrie if we
wanted to go live on the six o'clock broadcast for forty-five seconds and give an interview about "What Life is Like as a Superchav" I decided I'd wait till the cameras were filming and tell him
exactly what I thought. Go and look on YouTube — the clip is up
already. His face is a proper picture.

SATURDAY 27TH SEPTEMBER

9AM — Ms. Bracket has just sent me a text message saying that Mr. Bamblebury wants to see me in his office at 8:30AM SHARP on Monday morning to discuss my comments about Mayflower Academy.

Oh my days. Now I'm in SERIOUS BOTHER.

OCTOBER

WEDNESDAY 1ST OCTOBER

Clinton Brunton-Fletcher is not dead. IT'S OFFICIAL. But he's not living at Thundersley Road anymore either. Uma says he's "gone away for a bit." Uma didn't say where but I reckon Portsmouth as that's where the bloke he calls his dad lives. It said on the news tonight that there definitely was a gun fired outside Mayflower, but whoever fired it probably just fired one shot up into the air then drove off right away. The evening news said police are investigating claims that drugs are being sold around the school gates, which is "fueling gang tension."

So I go to my appointment with Mr. Bamblebury on Monday, and sit on a hard chair that hurts my arse amongst his dying potted plants and he starts quizzing me about Clinton Brunton-Fletcher and saying like, was Clinton really drug dealing, 'cos he'd heard this from several parents who were all calling up giving him an earache.

So I said, "I don't know NOTHING!" and I said it loud 'cos the honest to God truth is that I don't know much and what I do know for sure is that I'm no bloody grass. I mean WHAT'S IT GOT TO DO WITH ME if a gang of rudes want to roll up the school acting like big men? What's it got to do with me if Clinton wants to sell weed? For once in my life I was in the headmaster's office for something that had NOTHING to do with me at all! I just wanna read *King Lear.*

Mr. Bamblebury said all this *has* got something to do with me, 'cos I can HELP. Mr. Bamblebury said that Mayflower Academy is on the brink of turning a corner and it's important that we stay focused and on a positive track.

So I said, "WELL I'M STAYING POSITIVE, didn't you see me on BBC news?! I was representing big time, mate!"

So Mr. Bamblebury said, "Yes, Shiraz, thank you, and your comments were very spirited . . . although there was no need to call Max Blackford an ignorant-ass knobhead, was there?"

"Yeah, sorry 'bout that, Mr. Bamblebury," I said. "I got a bit worked up."

Mr. Bamblebury said that the Mayflower Sixth Formers already hold a "considerably weighty influence" around the school and that we needed to "take prime advantage" of this and "set a good example." So I said, "What does that mean in normal English?" and that's when Ms. Bracket stepped in and said that maybe the Sixth Formers could think about starting a little "Increase the Peace" campaign? Maybe I could plan a little assembly telling the Year Sevens to Elevens about the dangers of becoming involved with gangs and weapons and persuading them to go to Sixth Form instead and "be just like me."

BE JUST LIKE ME!?

I stared at them both like they were a pair of mentals for a bit. Then I said, "Eh? Why me? Why do I have to do it?" and Mr. Bamblebury said that the great thing about me was that I could really speak to the kids "at their level" and get through to them. Mr.

Bamblebury said most of the time he can't understand what any of the kids are even saying, like earlier that day he'd heard some Year Seven boy shouting, "Dat Bracket woman is nang, bruv" and he didn't know whether to tell him off as he didn't know what "nangbruv" was.

So I told Mr. Bamblebury that "nang" was good 'cos it means Ms. Bracket is good, she's like, cool. Mr. Bamblebury looked proper pleased then. Then he said that he'd also heard that the Year Tens had all started calling him "Mr. Bumbleclot" instead of Mr. Bamblebury and he didn't know whether that was a good or bad thing either? And at that point I decided to do the "Increase the Peace" campaign for Mr. Bamblebury 'cos to be honest I felt a bit sorry for him.

FRIDAY 3RD OCTOBER — SHIRAZ BAILEY WOOD'S BIRTHDAY!

I am seventeen today. Seventeen! Proper ancient! I thought seventeen might feel different, like suddenly I'd wake up feeling well mature and start watching *Emmerdale* and enjoying brussels sprouts and doing word-searches but it ain't like that at all. Seventeen just feels like sixteen.

When do you suddenly start feeling like a grown-up, I wonder? When do you suddenly get all your grown-up brain cells and know whether you're doing the right thing with your life and where you're going? When does that all come?

I asked my mother about it this morning and she said the moment she knew she was a grown-up was this day in the early '90s when she found herself in ShopRite in Romford and Cava-Sue had just started school and I was only a toddler and Murphy was just born and her mum had just died and suddenly she was in charge of everybody and she still felt like a kid herself but she weren't no more and she was staring at this packet of rice pudding like her mum used to make her and she realized she didn't know how to cook it and there was no one to tell her anymore and she had a panic attack and the manager had to take her to his office and make her a cup of sweet tea.

"Anyway," my mother said, chucking me a card in an envelope. "Don't worry about that now. Happy Birthday." Mum gave me a card on behalf of everyone in the family with a £20 gift card for TJ Maxx, then my Wesley came round tonight and took me out to Pizza Hut.

Wesley bought me a gold bracelet from Elizabeth Duke which sort of matches my locket. He is such a nice person. It's proper chunky though. "'Ere, Mum," I said to her once he'd gone. "You don't think this is a bit too bling if I wear it with the locket and the hoops is it?"

"Don't be soft," Mum said, "You can't never wear too much gold."

MONDAY 6TH OCTOBER

I've started recruiting people to take part in the Mayflower Academy: Increase the Peace campaign. Well, when I say "recruiting" what I mean is I stood on a chair in the Sixth Form common room today and said, "'Ere, everyone, listen!" and told them what Mr. Bamblebury wanted. Everyone just stared at me pulling the same "Are you a mentalist?" face that I did last week.

Finally Sean Burton, who was spending his study hall sewing glitter patches onto a silver bomber jacket to go and see Kylie Minogue, spoke up and said, "Shizza, have you seen some of those kids out there? There's one lad in Year Ten who calls himself Meatman who's got gold teeth and a tattoo of Tupac Shakur on his arm? He shouts 'Kill da fairy!' everytime he sees me!" Lots of folks nodded like they knew him. "Y'know, Shiz," Sean said, "I ain't overly concerned with increasing Meatman's peace. In fact, I'm sort of hoping someone shoots him soon."

"Thank you, Sean, that's ever so helpful," I said, although to be honest I could see his point. I started to panic a bit then. What the bloody hell was I going to do? But suddenly, Joshua Fallow stands up and says, "OK, Shiraz Bailey Wood, put my name down. I want to increase the peace!"

So I say, "Are you serious, Joshua?"

And he says, "Yeah, it's a good idea. We should do something. . . . I'll help you organize it. Just tell me what you want to do and I'll do it."

I wrote his name down and gave him a little smile 'cos despite him being proper up himself he had totally saved my life. Joshua gave me little wink and I felt a bit funny.

Of course, the moment Joshua says he'll help, lots of other people like Saf and Sean and Luther and Sonia and Carrie said they'd get involved too. We are the "Mayflower Academy: Increase the Peace Initiative."

Crapping hell — now we really have to do it.

Studying at my house is proper impossible. IMPOSSIBLE! I've told our Murphy a thousand times that he can't play bloody Dubstep in his room when I'm reading my Shakespeare but he just don't get it at all. I hate him sometimes.

In the end I went over to Carrie's house as we're supposed to have finished *Henry IV* Part One by tomorrow. Carrie wasn't much use at all. In fact she was a proper distraction. When I got to Draperville, Carrie was lying on her bed staring at the beauty section of *In Touch*.

Carrie said that eyes are going to be very big news next spring/summer season NOT lips like in autumn/winter. So I said, "Bloody hell, Cazza! You love your cupid-bow lips! What are you going to do!?" So Carrie says, "Doesn't matter, Shizzle, I'm going to start doing smudge kohl eyes instead like Tabitha Tennant did at the *TV Quick* awards."

So I said, "Wooo, dat is well nang, Cazza, but do you think we should read *Henry IV* Part One now?"

And Carrie said "Mmm . . . yeah, but first, what do you reckon about Saf? Do you reckon he'll end up snogging me if we do "Increase the Peace" campaign together? Man, he is well choong!"

The only time Carrie really picked up her Shakespeare was when we heard her dad on the landing shouting, "Carrie? I'm back!" Barney walked in and saw Carrie pretending to study and looked really happy. "Would the future CEO of Draper Hydration and her best friend fancy some Chinese food? 'Cos I'm putting a takeaway order in," he asked.

"Ooh thank you, Dad!" Carrie said. "Can me and Shiz share a Set Meal A? But change the pork balls to chicken in black beans and get shrimp crackers too. . . . THANK YOU DAD, YOU'RE THE BEST!"

The second he shut the door she picked up *In Touch* again and started reading an article called "Hollywood Tips for Heavenly Eyelashes."

FRIDAY 10TH OCTOBER

We had our first "Increase the Peace" meeting today in the Audio Visual room. I was well nervous 'cos I've never been in charge of anything before EVER and suddenly loads of Sixth Formers are all up in my face expecting me to have a plan and be all responsible. SCARY MARY.

Luckily Joshua Fallow showed up and he was proper confident and had loads of ideas in a folder with a sticker on it that said "INCREASE THE PEACE." Joshua had even been on the Internet and found this video by this bloke from Hackney called Wootbouy for a track called "Rude, U R Dead to Me." He made it as part of an anti-violence initiative just like ours.

The video is about how easy it is to start rolling with a gang and end up putting your whole family's life at risk. The video starts all exciting with boys and girls all dressed going to a shubz having a laugh and getting off with each other acting like mini-gangsters but then suddenly things start to get proper heavy with people getting shot and it ends up well upsetting with mums screaming by hospital beds and police dragging away one kid to jail after someone's been killed over some stupid beef over a stolen iPod. HEAVY.

We're going to show the Year Sevens to Elevens the video, then do a skit about how to "walk away from violence" and "increase the peace" then finally we're going to give some little speeches about how we all ended up in Mayflower Sixth Form and how bloody whoop-di-doo fantastic it is.

I don't know if I'll give a speech about that 'cos I'm scared my face might give away that Sixth Form is actually proper hard. In fact it's just like normal school but ten times harder with the added stress of finding a smart-caj outfit every morning.

Carrie has wangled her way into playing Saf's girlfriend in the skit. Luther, Joshua, and Sean are playing the part of a street gang who give Saf a well bad diss in Ilford Mall Burger King by saying something 'bout his mum. The skit is about whether Saf responds or just walks away and ignores them and "increases the peace." I'm the play's director.

The problem I see is that Luther isn't very scary at all (he's more cuddly 'cos all that weed he smokes gives him munchies so he's gotten quite fat), and Joshua talks like a proper posh boy and Sean is insisting on playing his part as a gangster wearing navy mascara and a silver bomber jacket with glitter Kylie Minogue patches. Oh bloody hell.

Luther's gang is totally wack. My nan and Clement could beat them up.

The whole thing would be bare jokes if I wasn't in charge of it all. We're performing to Year Seven on Monday! I hope I get squashed by a bus before then so I won't have to do it.

MONDAY 13TH OCTOBER

Today we did our first "Increase the Peace" assembly for Year Sevens.

I had been PROPER DREADING it all weekend. So much so that when Wesley took me to Fat Freddy's Foodstop at Romford Plaza this Saturday night I could hardly eat my buffalo wings or nothing and I didn't even smile when the waitresses were juggling stuff and tap dancing between courses which is the best thing about Fat Freddy's Foodstop (well, so Wesley reckons).

"It ain't just a restaurant, it's like seeing a show or something, innit," Wesley always says when we go. To be honest, I don't really like it. I just feel a bit sorry for the folks who work there. At least Mario just lets me serve fried egg rolls with my gob shut and I don't have to do two bloody verses of "Genie in a Bottle" by Christina Aguilera to get my tip. Wesley got a bit huffy when I told him that. He gets a bit huffy with me a lot these days.

"You weren't even watching them proper!" Wesley said. "You're always miles away these days, innit!" This made me a bit cross.

I felt like shouting, "Well maybe if you'd spent two hours after school watching Sean Burton running round in a neon crop-top and mascara carrying a bread knife shouting stuff like, 'Ooooh, take that bruv! Ya just got merked!' while Saf rolled about on the floor laughing not looking dead at all and Carrie painted her nails and read *US Weekly,* well YOU'D WANT TO BE MILES AWAY TOO!" But I didn't say that I just shrugged and said I was sorry.

Anyway, after all that, our assembly sort of went OK. Well more than "sort of." Mr. Bamblebury reckoned it was "a roaring success." Basically, we turn up in the hall at 9:30AM today and the Year Seven kids all arrived at once and started sitting on the floor with their legs crossed looking proper excited. The Year Sevens are well tiny and quite sweet. I don't ever remember me and Carrie being so small and cute-looking but we must have been I suppose.

We turned all the lights off and it was totally dark and silent aside from the odd fart and giggle, then we put on the Wootbouy video for them all to watch. They all watched it proper quietly without saying a single word to each other and by the bit where it got all heavy with the blood and folks dying and stuff I looked at the front row and some little girls were almost crying and the boys looked proper scared.

Then we put the lights back on and we did our little play and everyone — Saf, Luther, Joshua, Sean, and Carrie — all tried proper hard to do it well and no one forgot their lines and none of the little kids seemed to notice how flouncy Sean is or that Joshua sounds posh like Prince Harry or that Luther would be more dangerous as a gang member if he ditched the knife and just sat on people and squashed them with his big bum instead.

Then Joshua stood up and said a little speech about how amazing Sixth Form is and all the little girls in the room just stared at his face and wide shoulders with their mouths wide open listening to every word like they were proper madly in love and then he got them to shout "LET'S ALL INCREASE THE PEACE!" all at the same time together and he asked if they would ever get involved with gangs and violence and they all shouted "NOOOOOOOO!" and he asked whether they'd try to stay on in Sixth Form and they all said "YESSSSSSS!" then they all left to go to class and Mr. Bamblebury looked proper happy and said he was "over the moon with this very valuable work."

So I got home tonight and I felt sort of happy for a bit then I put on the news and it said that some kid over in Streatham had been stabbed to death after school tonight by four other kids on the number 45 bus in what was being described by police as a "post-school scuffle."

I sat for a bit and cuddled Penny and I thought about how mental everything is in this world and felt a bit sad 'cos in the grand scheme of things me and Joshua and Carrie and the gang probably hadn't increased much peace at all.

WEDNESDAY 15TH OCTOBER

I went to bingo tonight with Nan and Clement. It's funny going places with them 'cos they are proper old and think about everything in a different way than young people do. They don't ever get too stressed about nothing like guns or knives or gangs or respect or homework grades or how Martin Luther changed the face of organized religion in the 14th century or whether or not Shakespeare meant to portray Henry IV as lazy or whether no one has left them any MySpace messages or what sort of lipstick Tabitha Tennant is wearing or how fat or thin they look in their sensible cardigans. They never think about nothing like that. It must be quite good fun being old.

All they're into is bingo, bowling, crosswords, nice cups of tea, and having a laugh. "Ain't nothing in this life much worth shooting each other over," my nan said when I told her about the "Increase the Peace" campaign.

"No, that's not true," said Clement sounding proper serious, "I'd shoot a man clean between the ears if he tried to keep me from one of your sponge cakes." Then Clement winked at Nan and they both laughed proper loud like kids and Nan poked Clement for teasing her and he poked her back just like you'd do if you fancied each other a bit which I'm sure they don't. Nan won £50 in bingo and they put her name on the big screen and gave her a cheer so it was well exciting.

It took my mind a bit off today's assembly we did for Years Eight and Nine. I mean, it went OK and everything, but it just wasn't the same as the one we did for Year Seven. It was as if the Year Eights and Nines weren't properly listening. They were just there 'cos they had to be. And when Joshua got them to shout out the stuff at the end they did it sort of half-heartedly and some of them never answered at all.

"I think you gave them so many ideas to think about you stunned them into silence!" said Mr. Bamblebury afterward.

Mmm. Yeah.

FRIDAY 17TH OCTOBER

OH MY GOSH. Today was proper humiliating. My face is still red just writing this. So today we did our "Increase the Peace" assembly for the Year Tens and Elevens. Well, actually just Year Tens as hardly no Year Elevens showed up as they were all doing homework or were just skiving or they didn't know it was happening or were pretending not to know or couldn't be arsed. BRILLIANT.

So me, Carrie, Saf, Sean, Joshua, Nabila, Luther, and all the rest of us are waiting in the hall and the Year Tens start arriving, mooching in slowly with folded arms and scowls on their faces like they don't want to be there one little bit. Right away some lairy girls wearing mini-skirts start shouting stuff out at us and trying to come over and mess with our projector and some of the boys are asking what "all this crap" is about, then laugh at us when we explain. I felt proper angry then and wanted to kick off but Joshua put his arm around my waist and told me to chill. For some reason, I did what he said. My heart felt all fluttery when he touched me, but it was probably just nerves.

Then Murphy comes in with Tariq and some other really tall boys and I waved at him and the little shit pretended not to know me!!! Then a couple of boys in the back row started having a fight and Ms. Bracket had to split them up and tell everyone really sternly to CALM DOWN NOW. Then, just as we were about to begin, Mr. Bamblebury stormed in with about seven really tall, scary-looking boys who had half-grown mustaches and hoodies and baseball caps and nothing like proper uniforms on and he shouted, "Right, you sit near the front! You should hear this so LISTEN UP GOOD!"

Right away I figured that one of them was Meatman and another one was Delano and I dunno who the rest were but they looked like a right bunch of rudes even though I'm pretty sure there never used to be any rudes in Murphy's year at all. Just spotty little boys in blazers too big for them who'd never DARE give no one in our year any trouble at all. WHAT HAPPENED TO THEM? When did they all get so ginormous? Meatman sat down on the front row and took one look at all of us and chucked his head back and laughed. Then he folded his arms and glared at Sean and pretended to cough but said "fairy." Then he sucked his gold teeth in a proper dramatic way like he was showboating and everyone laughed and some people even clapped.

I felt well sorry for Sean then 'cos his hands were shaking. I felt irate too 'cos what bloody right has anyone got to make anyone feel like that? I mean what if Sean is maybe a bit, well, gay? He ain't harming no one. Sean's not the one with the crap tattoo and a mouth like my nan's bloody cheese-grater. I wanted to shout that at Meatman 'cos he ain't no big man he's a bloody overgrown fifteen-year-old child thinking he's some sort of rude but I thought it might end up like that bit in the *Incredible Hulk* movie when Hulk starts picking folks up and whirling them round his head shouting, "Hulky angry! Hulky smash!"

So we put the lights off and put the video on and at first everyone just talked but they shut up once the scenes started where the kids are dealing drugs and riding about in Escalades and Benz Jeeps drinking champagne and getting all up in each other's faces in nightclub VIP rooms and being all gangster. Meatman and Delano and the rest of the audience seemed to really like this. They were cheering and pretending to fire guns at the screen.

Then the video moved on to where kids start getting shot and stabbed and the parents start getting involved and kids are crying in apartment stairwells and bodies are on mortuary slabs and police are shoving people in jail cells and it gets proper heavy.

I looked at the Year Tens and I see that Meatman had got bored now and got his phone out and he's sending a text and Delano is chatting up some girl near him and everyone had got a bit distracted; even my bloody brother Murphy was talking to Tariq.

It was like the end scenes were just going right over their heads. They didn't care at all. They probably see this type of thing every day on MTV, so it weren't like any big deal to them. Then the lights went on and Ms. Bracket saw us Sixth Formers were a bit flustered so she stepped in and said "So, has anyone got any comments about this video?" and everyone just pretended to be deaf or ignored her.

Then Meatman said, "I got a comment, Miss. Can we watch the first half again 'cos all the gangster bit was well nang before all the preaching crap started."

Then Delano chipped in with, "Man, dat blood was asking to get merked anyway."

Then lots of the boys in the front row laughed well loud and fired invisible guns in the air shouting, "Brap Brap Braaaap!"

I won't even describe what happened during our play. It is still proper painful in my brain. All I'll say is the image of Meatman chasing Sean through the assembly hall in a salmon-pink bolero jacket with glitter patches while a group of Year Tens shouted, "Run Fairy Run! Ruuuuuuuuun!" will stay in my head forever.

MONDAY 20TH OCTOBER

Meatman has been suspended from Mayflower Academy for two weeks.

I called Sean today and told him. Sean was in bed watching Season One of *The OC* on DVD and eating string cheese and feeling proper suicidal.

Sean says he ain't never coming out of his house again until he knows he ain't under threat or nothing. So I says, "Oh, come back Sean, I'll be your bodyguard. I ain't scared of Meatman."

Then Sean laughed a bit and says, "I know you're not scared of him, you loon. You're proper hard as nails you are, princess."

Sean says he'll come back sometime soon but not today 'cos he's bleaching his hair. I felt happier when he said he was bleaching his hair 'cos no one bothers to spend an hour wrapped in tinfoil just to kill themselves, do they?

Mr. Bamblebury and Ms. Bracket say we shouldn't be discouraged by the near riot that broke out in our final "Increase the Peace" assembly. Mr. Bamblebury says, "All great journeys start with a few small steps."

So I said, "Well, tell Sean Burton that, Mr. Bamblebury, 'cos he took more than a few small steps, in fact, he was well past the supermarket hiding in a Dumpster when I found him." Joshua snorted Fanta down his nose when I said that.

Mr. Bamblebury just pretended to be deaf. He can't handle me being real. I always keep it real. Joshua says my rap name would be MC Realize.

WEDNESDAY 22ND OCTOBER

Carrie and Saf are going out together! They were working after school last night on some geography homework and Saf asked Carrie if he could have a snog and Carrie said yes and she gave him a quick snog but that was all so she reckons, although they are both now banned from the library for a week and the librarian has put a lock on the reserved book room closet.

Carrie and Saf are well loved-up together. They roll around on the common room sofas, cleaning out each other's ears with their mouths and pawing each other. Joshua Fallow says it's like refereeing one long World Wrestling Entertainment Smackdown. Joshua is bare jokes sometimes even though he is quite posh.

I went and ate my Chicken Chow Mein outside today 'cos of all the squelching. Me and my Wesley are never really like that. Not even when we first got off. We are more like best friends. I mean, it ain't normal all that squelching, is it?

FRIDAY 24TH OCTOBER

Thank flaming God it is Friday. This week has been proper hardcore. I've had English homework and films to watch and history books to read and peace to increase and Sean Burton to bodyguard and my head is in a proper spin. I don't know how I'm supposed to fit so much into one girl's brain.

Wesley knows I am proper stressed so he said he'd take me down Romford for happy hour at Pizza Junction, that place where you sit in a booth that's like a racing car and traffic lights flash on and off and horns honk at your table when your order is ready. It's quite a laugh, even if all the noise and flashing does sometimes gives me a migraine.

Wesley and me shared a Sloppy Joe pizza and a hot chocolate fudge cake and Wesley was telling me 'bout this lad Wazzle on his plumbing NVQ who flooded this posh woman in Epping Forest's bathroom and I was trying to tell Wesley about history where we're learning about Renaissance architects and how they started building churches ginormously massive in the 14th century to make the people feel like they were properly in the presence of God, but Wesley didn't really get what I was going on about so I sort of gave up.

On the way home Wesley said he had something to show me and I thought, "Oh here goes, it'll be something in a store window." But it wasn't at all it was something much bigger than that.

We drove back to Thundersley Road on the route that goes past Bishop Fledding Industrial Estate where I once did some work experience in a Indian food factory. Round the back of the park there's a building site with a big sign that says LUXURY HOMES AVAILABLE SOON.

So Wesley parks the car and puts on some hip-hop and I sat for a bit listening to the words to "Kill You When I'm Dead" by Mazzio and my mind started wandering to Meatman and the Year Tens.

"'Ere, Wesley, don't you think this gangster rap stuff is sort of bad for, like, society?" I said. But Wesley just looks at me funny and says, "But we don't live in America, Shiraz! It ain't nothing like as bad as this in Essex." So I shut up about that and asked what it was he wanted to show me then.

"Look at those condos they're building, innit," he said. "I think they're proper nice."

I looked at them and I said, "Well, yeah, they're gonna be well good when they're finished, why, what's so special about them?"

And Wesley says, "Well, if you think about it, they're exactly halfway between your mum's and my mum's houses, innit?"

So I says, "Yeah, I suppose."

And Wesley says, "Well, the thing is, Shizza, y'know when my dad died he left me a little bit of money, innit? Just a little bit, mind. Well my nan put it in a bank account for me and she's been adding to it here and there for about eighteen years with bingo wins and that and on my birthdays and . . . well the thing is, there's a few grand now and I reckon if I get a job straight after my NVQ, I reckon I might have enough for a down payment on one of them condos, innit."

I looked over at the building site which was full of cement mixers and rubble.

"You wanna live in one of them condos?" I said.

"Well, not just me," he says, "Me and you, innit. You'd come and live with me too, wouldn't you, and help me with the mortgage?

In a few years, mind, when you finish all this school stuff and you get a job in Ilford?"

"I'd move in with you?" I said.

"Yeah," he said. "I want us to be together forever, innit."

I didn't know what to say. I've never ever thought seriously of leaving Thundersley Road and if I have it wasn't to move into a condo five minutes away.

Thing is, I've not really properly thought EVER about what I'm gonna do with my life. I only got as far as signing up for Sixth Form. I haven't figured out any other stuff about the next seventy years!!!

"You want us to live together in a condo in Goodmayes? Forever?" I said.

"Well, not right now," he said, "But someday soon. I love you, Shiraz."

I looked at him for a bit and he got hold of my hand and held it tight.

"I love you too, Wesley." I said, and I properly meant it.

But at the same time I sort of didn't.

NOVEMBER

TUESDAY 4TH NOVEMBER

It's weird 'cos Wesley's never mentioned that condo behind Bishop Fledding Industrial Estate since that night last month. Neither have I.

It's a bit like Wesley reckons me and him have made some sort of secret pact to move in together which we totally haven't 'cos I totally didn't say yes at all. All I said was, "Mmmm, dunno, Wes. That's a lot to think about." Then I made him drive me home quick 'cos my mother wanted to borrow his superplunger to unblock hair from the upstairs sink.

I wasn't lying. It IS a lot to think about. And believe me, the last thing Shiraz Bailey Wood needs right now is something else that makes her have to think 'cos her brain is bloody FULL up with other stuff like flipping AS-Level Critical Thinking.

OH MY GOSH that whole course is one ginormous headbend. Basically you get a question that is totally easy like, "Should pedophiles go to jail?" which is a proper no brainer 'cos the answer is "YES, RIGHT AWAY" but then you have a "debate about morals and ethics" then suddenly it's not so straightforward no more and before you know it you're sounding like you're the one bloody sticking up for pedophiles and everyone in the class has fallen out and the bell goes and you've got a sore throat from shouting and a pain behind one eye and some homework to do for 9AM tomorrow. BRILLIANT.

Today we talked about cars and pollution. Joshua Fallow started arguing that all cars should cost double the price to stop road congestion. Saf and Manpreet told him to shut up and stop being a tree-hugger. Then Joshua went a bit further and said he would ban all modded cars with rims and stupid extra-loud chavvy stereos to stop chavsters from making fools of themselves. Everyone started laughing well loud then and I could feel my cheeks go hot 'cos my Wesley has got glowing wheel arches and they do look a bit silly though I'd never tell him.

Then Joshua said when he is Prime Minister he's bringing in long jail sentences for anyone caught attending Dagenham car meets in a souped-up Golf with munter girlfriends who keep flashing their norks to get in *Super Street* car magazine. And by this point everyone in the class was proper howling INCLUDING me 'cos Wesley's ex-bird Dee Dee used to go up to Dagenham looking like a right old hoochie with her schnockers out like cow's udders.

Joshua Fallow is bare jokes sometimes. If Joshua said come and live in a condo behind an industrial estate with me forever I'd probably say OK, 'cos he's not just well choong to look at, the conversation would be exciting too.

10PM — Oh God. I can't believe I just wrote that. See that's what Critical Thinking does to your head. **IT MAKES YOUR BRAIN PLAY TRICKS ON YOU.**

WEDNESDAY 5TH NOVEMBER

CRAP CRAP CRAP. I think me and Wesley might have had our first proper serious argument like what you hear relationship experts talk about on morning shows. We don't normally ever get into arguments 'cos we're like best friends but tonight was different.

So, OK, this is my fault probably 'cos I am proper stressed out with studying but tonight I'm in my room trying to write an essay about this fat alco bloke called Falstaff in the Shakespeare play *Henry IV* Part One when I hear our Staffy barking its head off downstairs and Murphy shouting, "All right, Wes, wanna play *Killerquest?*" and my mother trying to force-feed Wes a boiled tongue sandwich that I know she got on quick sale down at ShopRite and Cava-Sue sticking her beak in about factory farming. Basically, there's a lot of noise AS BLOODY USUAL.

So I go downstairs and say, "Wesley, what you doing here? I'm studying tonight!"

And he says, "Yeah, you said you'd study for a bit!"

And I say "Nah . . . I said I was studying all night, I'm doing homework! Homework is IMPORTANT!" And Wesley sort of rolled his eyes and everyone sighed like I was being proper tight, so I storm into the kitchen and Wesley follows and tries to give me a cuddle and I shook him off and said, "You want me to fail my A-Levels, don't you!" which WAS proper tight, I admit.

So Wesley says, "Course I don't! I was just passing so I popped in!"

So I says, "Well, DON'T JUST POP IN when I got work to do!"

And Wesley looked proper hurt then and he picks up his car keys and storms out of the door and drives off well fast.

"Oh, well done, Shiraz!" my mother shouted, "Go on! Scare him off! You'll not get another one like him! You'll end up like your Auntie Annie, you will! She was always scaring men off! Wanting her own way! Where's she now? Living on her own in Hastings with three cats and a grumbling ovary!"

I stormed through the living room and up the stairs then got under the cover and pulled it over my head and fumed.

I ain't apologizing. Us Wood women NEVER do.

SATURDAY 8TH NOVEMBER

Me and my Wesley are still not speaking. I know we will soon 'cos it don't feel like we've split up or nothing. We're just having a break on account of him doing my head right in big time.

I was just reading Cava-Sue's *Marie Claire* magazine on the loo and it said, "All relationships need space to breathe sometimes" which I reckon is totally right. I need space all right, lots of it, this house is doing my nut in.

So I come home from Mr. Yolk tonight and I'm just halfway up the path when the front door swings open and my Aunty Glo trots out going, "Ooh, Shiraz, you're in for a treat tonight! I brought round my karaoke machine and my new *Singalonga-Motown Classics* CD! Do you want stuff from the liquor store? Breezer or nothing?"

"No, you're all right," I said, gritting my teeth and walking into the living room where my mother was tuning up her vocal chords to "Love Really Hurts Without You" and my dad was in his chair eating chicken curry and fries out of the carton 'cos he often gets himself a takeaway on the way home from Goodmayes Social on Saturday afternoon and he'd dribbled curry sauce down his T-shirt and he looked like a bloody homeless. "Ooh all right lovey!" shouted my mother into the microphone, "Look what your Aunty Glo has brought us round!"

"Brilliant," I said.

Aunty Glo ain't my real aunty by the way. She's just my mum's mate who used to work with her when Mum was a cleaner years ago. I was describing Glo to Joshua Fallow the other day and he said he's got randoms like that in his family too. Like this one bloke he calls Uncle Zac who works at the *Guardian* newspaper who ain't his uncle at all, he's just someone his dad was on crew with at the university.

I shut up after that. I didn't want Josh to ask how my mum met Aunty Glo.

So anyway, I'm standing there watching my mother murdering "Ain't No Mountain High Enough" and thinking, "SO MUCH FOR BLOODY STUDYING TONIGHT," when suddenly my phone vibrates in my pocket.

It was a text. A text from Uma Brunton-Fletcher.

U dn the Shkspr essay yet? Uma said.

I looked at it for a bit. Then typed back.

Not yt. 2nite. May B.

My phone bleeped again.

Wn 2 come and study at mine? it said.

Do I want to study with Uma Brunton-Fletcher?

I looked at my mother's big mouth flapping open and shut.

OK — B rnd in 30 minuts. I typed.

Walking down to Uma's carrying the *Complete Works of Shake-speare* under my arm felt proper weird. I felt embarrassed to be honest 'cos I've hardly spoke to Uma or nothing much in Sixth Form. I've been treating her a bit like everyone else does. Like I don't really know why she's there. I feel tight about that now. I didn't even ask her to be in the "Increase the Peace" campaign, which was well shady, 'cos if anyone knows anything about rudes and violence and getting dragged into stuff it's Uma.

I knocked on Uma's door and stood for a while by the aban-doned fridge and overturned shopping cart while Uma opened the six separate locks on her front door, and I'm thinking, "Great, this is all I need, I'm already bloody confused about Shakespeare, now I'm going to have to waste my Saturday night explaining it all to one of the biggest superchavs in Goodmayes." Which is tight I know but I was in a bad mood.

"Y'all right," said Uma.

"Y'all right," I said, then I went inside.

Uma's house was proper silent. No music or no family, no nothing. No one lives there any more except for Uma and Zeus. The whole place was proper clean and tidy. The kitchen was as neat as anything. Nothing like when her stepdad used to sell skunk. I sat on the sofa and enjoyed the total silence for a bit. Uma sat on the big chair, picked up a laptop, and plonked it on her knee.

"Hang on a sec, Shiz, I'm just playing poker. I'm up three hundred quid today so far," she said, peering at the screen.

"You got WiFi broadband?!" I said, trying not to sound shocked.

"Next-door neighbors have," said Uma. "They don't put no password on it though."

I laughed. Some things never change.

"Hang on," I said. "Ain't that one of the school's laptops that got nicked last year?!"

Uma cringed a bit.

"Oh don't bloody ask," she groaned. "It was my Christmas present from Clinton."

I took my trainers off and curled up on the sofa with Zeus cuddled into my legs and started reading my book. Uma finished her poker game and got us both a drink and then started surfing the Net looking for sites with AS-Level answers on "just to help us out a bit."

"Where's Carrie tonight?" said Uma, fiddling with her clown pendant and lighting up an Marlboro Red.

"With Saf, I reckon. She's well loved up," I said.

"Dat Saf is well choong though, innit," said Uma, sighing a bit.

"Yep," I said, "She's well lucky."

Uma thought for a bit.

"Dat Joshua is buff though too, ain't he?" she said.

"Erm . . . I ain't ever noticed really," I said. Fibbing like anything.

Uma smiled to herself, then she goes, "I reckon Joshua Fallow is well into you, man."

"Nah. No way," I said, and my stomach felt all squelchy.

Uma stared at the screen for a while. Then she said, "Carrie

Draper is proper blessed tho, ain't she? She's well lucky having that minted rich dad and that, ain't she? She could have all his business one day if she wanted."

I laughed a bit. Uma was bang on the money there.

"I dunno if she does want it though," I said.

"Yeah," said Uma, tapping her ciggie ashes in her cup, and blowing smoke down her nostrils, "She's just like that Prince Hal in *Henry IV* Part One ain't she? Y'know when Hal's dad the King is jarring his head for him to buck his ideas up? That's what this whole play's about ain't it? It's about everything being there on a plate for you, but you can't be bloody arsed."

I looked at Uma for a bit then I started to laugh again.

"Yeah, it is a bit isn't it?" I said.

We're studying together later this week.

WEDNESDAY 12TH NOVEMBER

If you were to say, "Shiz, have you missed Wesley Barrington Bains II during your week-long break?" Well I'd be proper confused as to how to answer.

'Cos on one hand I ain't missed having Wesley turning up distracting me and trying to get me to go to his house for some "private time" when his mum's out. Or not understanding when I talk about school. But at the same time, I've missed him a lot too. I know Wesley inside out and he knows me too. It's like one of the family has gone missing when he don't come round. That's why we've been texting a bit. Just silly jokes and stuff.

I got home from school tonight and my mother looked proper

happy and paused *Emmerdale* and she said, "There's someone waiting for you upstairs!!!!" So I said, "Is it Wesley Barrington Bains II?"

And Mum went, "Go and have a look." So I went up to my room and I COULDN'T believe my eyes.

On the bed in my tiny bedroom was an absolutely ginormous teddy bear. Massive. EXTRA EXTRA HUGE!! The sort of bear so big they have to put a sign beside it in Clinton's Card Shop in Romford telling folks to stop their kiddies climbing on it.

It's brown and fluffy with a red T-shirt on that says I LOVE YOU BABY in big white letters. I couldn't believe my eyes. I tried moving it on the floor but it was too heavy and there was no bloody space to anyway.

So I call up Wesley and I go, "Wesley, are you some sort of mental or something?"

And he laughs and says, "Well, yeah, maybe I am, you drive me proper mental."

And I go, "What have you put this bear in my room for?"

And he says, "'Cos I want us to stop having the hump with each other, eh? I love you, Shiraz Bailey Wood." My lip wobbled a bit when he said that.

"I love you too," I said.

So we decided to stop having the hump. And we decided that maybe one of our problems is that Wesley feels a bit left out now that I'm doing Mayflower Sixth Form and have got all new friends.

"Maybe if you let me join in more, things would be better," Wesley said.

"Maybe," I said.

I invited Wesley to come along to this quiz we're having at

school on Friday night to raise cash for the "Increase the Peace" campaign. We're trying to raise cash to buy the school music room a sampler and mini-mixing desk.

Joshua Fallow reckons that'll give the rudes something to distract them from jacking each other's phones and trainers for a bit. It's a good idea we all think.

I mean worst-case scenario: even if Meatman does get round to stabbing someone, at least now he can record a proper slamming track about it afterward.

FRIDAY 14TH NOVEMBER

Our quiz was a proper success! We raised three hundred quid! Uma Brunton-Fletcher offered to turn it into two grand overnight playing online poker, but we all reckoned it would be a better idea if we gave it to Joshua and he put it into the special Mayflower "Increase the Peace" bank account he set up last week.

Tonight was well funny 'cos loads of us Sixth Formers showed up and some people brought their mums or dads or grans and some people brought their girlfriends or boyfriends we'd never met before and some people brought their friends from other schools and it was a right old mix-up and everyone had a good laugh. Well, I think everyone did, I'm not too sure about Wesley. He didn't laugh much.

We put Manpreet in charge of questions 'cos he's a right old Asperger's case so at least we knew it would get done properly. Then we all got into teams. Me, Carrie, Saf, Wesley, and Joshua were on one team called "The Merklemen." Nabila Chaalan,

Sonia Cathcart, and Danny Braffman who is an Orthodox Jew were on a team called "The Holy Trinity." Sean and his clubbing mates Gaz and Jean-Paul were called "The Screaming Marys." I don't think my Wesley could believe Sean called his team that 'cos he looked a bit shocked but you just have to get used to stuff like that in Sixth Form. We're all individuals and you gotta live and let live.

"So you're the famous Wesley Barrington Bains II?" Joshua said to Wesley the second we all sat down.

"Er, yeah, that's me, innit," said Wesley.

"I'm Joshua Fallow," said Josh. "I've heard stacks about you."

Wesley looked at Joshua a bit funny. Wesley probably wasn't sure whether Josh was taking the piss or not.

To be honest, I'm never proper sure either. And the fact is I don't talk about Wesley that much at all at school, certainly not around Joshua, so he might've been being snarky.

"So, what's your specialist subject tonight, Wesley?" said Joshua.

"What?" said Wesley.

"What you into?" said Joshua.

"Erm, well, I'm into cars. Pimped cars. Modded cars. Car meets. That sort of thing, innit," said Wesley.

"Car meets?" said Joshua, sounding like he didn't know who was taking the mick out of who now.

I looked at them both; Joshua with his cheekbones in his baggy Box Fresh sweatshirt and floppy hair and low-rider cord combat trousers. Wesley in his Nike sweatshirt and Reebok classics and Von Dutch baseball cap. They looked like they were from different flaming planets.

"Yeah, Josh," said Carrie joining in. "Car meets! You should see Wesley's car! It's proper modded out. Glowing wheel arches and everything, hasn't it? We used to all go down Dagenham cruising in it, didn't we Wes, when I went out with Bezzie?"

Joshua's face didn't change. He didn't even smirk. But *my* face was burning up. For a few weird seconds I felt proper silly sitting there wearing my ginormous gold locket and gold bracelet with my boyfriend who goes to car meets. But then I caught hold of my head and thought, "No, that's who I am! I'm only keeping it real."

Wesley drove me home afterward. I asked him if he had a good time and he said it was OK, but he felt a bit thick 'cos even though The Merklemen won he didn't answer no questions. Wes said everyone was nice enough though, even though a few of them were a bit up themselves. I asked him who and he said "that Joshua." He says Joshua was OK and all that but he's just one of them rich kids who think they're it. Wesley says he can't stand folk like that.

"Yeah," I said. "Me neither."

WEDNESDAY 19TH NOVEMBER

Seventeen is turning out to be a right old headbend of an age. Here was me thinking it might be the year when I get closer to working out what I'm doing with my life. Instead, every day just makes me more confused.

So I'm sitting in the library today pretending to read about the Golden Age of Ferdinand and Isabella of Spain, except I'm not really. I'm listening to proper old-skool Wu Tang Clan on my cell phone and doodling a drawing of a fancy cat with a tiara on onto my notebook and staring out the window. All of a sudden a load of bags and files slam down on the desk and I look up and it's Saf and Josh and Carrie all swarming around me.

"Hard at it as usual," said Joshua, looking at my cat which for some reason had dangly earrings and buck teeth which I reckon, if it was analyzed by a head specialist might signal that I am some sort of nutjob.

"Aw, leave her, Josh," said Carrie. "Shizza works harder than all of us."

"Thank you, Carrie," I said, but by this point Carrie had her tongue halfway down Saf's throat and was pinching his bum at the same time.

"Oh, take it somewhere private!" groaned Joshua. "It's like watching feeding time at the bloody warthog pen."

The pair wandered off to look at books together.

Joshua sat down opposite me and stared right in my face.

"Mr. Bamblebury has bought a twelve-channel mixing board for the music room with our quiz money," he said.

"Flaming hell! That's good," I said. Josh nodded slowly.

"We should do another quiz or a raffle or something," Josh said. "We could make enough to get new mics and crap like that."

"Yeah," I said. Then I thought for a bit.

"Wow," I said. 'You proper care about all this 'Increase the Peace' thing don't you?"

Joshua looked at me, then he burst out laughing.

"No. I honestly couldn't give a crap," he said.

"So why are you doing all this then?" I said.

Joshua looked at me like I was a bit simple. "Shiraz, have you any idea how good all this charity stuff looks on your university application forms? Raising money? Helping the community? Don't say you didn't think about that too?"

My cheeks went a bit hot then.

"No, I didn't think about that. I've never thought nothing about university applications. I don't even think I'm going to university."

Joshua narrowed his eyes.

"What?" he said. "Why aren't you thinking about it? You SHOULD go to university. Why wouldn't you go?"

"Well, I dunno," I said, "I've never really imagined it. No one in my family has ever gone to uni. Dunno why."

Joshua thought for a few seconds, mulling it over.

"Well, that's just wack," he said. "What you going to do instead? Stay in Goodmayes? Marry that Wesley bloke with the modded car and the sovereign ring?"

I cringed when Joshua said that. I wish Wes had never worn that bloody ring to quiz night.

My face must have looked sad then 'cos Josh stopped being so pushy.

"Look, I'm not being tight, Shiraz," said Josh. "I'm just saying. You're clever. Really clever. And funny. And good fun."

"Thank you," I said.

"And pretty. And sexy. With a nice set of jugs."

"Joshua!" I said.

"Sorry, sorry. My special brain pills haven't kicked in today yet," he said. "My mouth is out of control."

I didn't say anything. I just looked at him and felt really squelchy and hot inside. Like I never feel with my Wesley.

"Hey, anyway," said Josh. "Has Ms. Bracket told you about the Christmas class trip yet?"

"No!" I said.

"We're going to see *King Lear* at the Globe theater on the Southbank in London."

My heart went boom when he said that. I love London. Ever since me and Wesley drove there alone last year it's always felt like it's there, eleven miles away being proper exciting without me.

"And then . . ." said Joshua. "And this is the unofficial, not Ms. Bracket bit, we're going clubbing afterward!"

"No! Straight up?" I said.

"True fact," said Joshua. "I'm sorting it out."

Then the bell started to ring for next class so we both began collecting our stuff. "And I hope you're coming, Shiraz Bailey Wood. 'Cos it's going to be Christmas and we're going to go partying. And it's going to be messy. And besides . . . I want my Christmas snog."

And with that he walked off leaving me more confused about life than I'd possibly ever been EVER.

DECEMBER

MONDAY 1ST DECEMBER

Oh God. I keep having bad dreams about Joshua Fallow ever since he said that stupid thing about my jugs which he probably never meant anyway, 'cos he is a proper player who flirts with everyone. Not scary dreams. Nice dreams. Ones I'm proper ashamed to describe.

Last night for example, I dreamed that Joshua Fallow was riding a horse wearing just his undercrackers through Ilford Mall and he starts chatting me up outside TopShop and he gets off his horse and his body is well buff and then he is biting my neck like a vampire then we are rolling about together in the flower beds doing what my Nan would probably describe as "heavy petting."

I woke up breathing all funny, with a big grin on my face and the duvet kicked off and my nightie all twisted, covered in sweat. That giant bear Wesley bought me was on the floor staring at me crossly like I'm some sort of hoochie mama.

I felt guilty, and it's not fair 'cos I'd NEVER cheat on my Wesley. NEVER. Not when I'm awake anyhow. But I can't bloody help who I snog in my sleep CAN I?

WEDNESDAY 3RD DECEMBER

Ooh, it's starting to feel proper Christmassy already! Carrie and Barney Draper have been getting the legendary Draperville Christmas lights display ready. This time it's gonna be BIGGER AND BETTER THAN EVER! They're doing the Santa's sleigh and Rudolph running up the front of the house and decorating the tree with a zillion flashing lights as usual and they're also doing a weird eight-foot-tall snowman with the mechanical moving arms and a flashing carrot nose . . . BUT THERE'S MORE! This year the Drapers have hired a life-sized nativity scene! With a baby Jesus in a manger being beheld by three wise men from afar and shepherds and everything!!!

It's not like Barney Draper is proper religious or anything. To be honest I reckon he's only doing the nativity 'cos the *Ilford Bugle* kept saying Essex council were going to ban the word "Christmas" 'cos of the word "Christ" being offensive. So now Barney's making a big point of celebrating Christ 'cos he says he's got a perfect right to and besides, "It's not like I started whining last Eid when Amjad at Number 39 and his lot were giving it the big one about Allah!"

I just nodded when Barney said that, then helped him hammer up some plywood to make a shelter for the baby Jesus and his whole team of plastic supporters, which included a sad praying woman, a bloke with a beard who looked like the magician David Blaine, a sheep, an ox, and some other weird biblical animals made from flame-retardant materials.

I asked Barney if there was any room in his biblical scene for a proper massive teddy bear so huge kiddies could clamber on it. Barney said, "Yeah, of course." He's picking up the bear tomorrow. THANK YOU GOD.

MONDAY 15TH DECEMBER

Oh my gosh it's the 15th already!! I ain't done none of my shopping! Not one present. Sonia Cathcart has done all of her Christmas shopping, fancy-wrapped it in special bows and got it all under her Christmas tree! "I'm sooooo glad I was organized this year!" Sonia Cathcart keeps saying. "I'd HATE to be rushing around!" she keeps saying. "Now I've got more time to party at Christmas," she keeps saying, 227 times a day.

"Oh shut it you annoying cow!" I feel like shouting, "You don't even know what partying is! You won't even risk drinking the Cup-a-Soup with the spicy croutons in your variety pack 'cos you reckon you've got food allergies and high blood pressure YOU SILLY BINT!" I don't say it though. I just think it.

All I've done so far is make a list:

Mum: CD of covers by Pop Idol winners.

Dad: 3-pack of vests from Macy's (dark color to hide curry stains).

Murphy: Page 3 Model Calendar from the supermarket.

Carrie: Tabitha Tennant Underarm Roll-on — "Pong-Gone by Tabitha T."

Cava-Sue and Lewis: A book about traveling TO REMIND THEM TO GO.

Penny: Cadbury's Chocolates box (large) and bag of Purina Lo-fat Science Diet.

Nan: One of them novels she likes with a picture of a woman in a Victorian bodice being groped by a geezer in riding jodhpurs on the front.

Clement: Entenmann's marble loaf cake.

I'll do all that after school one night.

11PM — Wesley! Oh God, I forgot about him: something from Best Buy or Sports Authority.

TUESDAY 16TH DECEMBER

Wesley's teddy bear is a big hit at the Draperville lights display!! Carrie's family have raised over a grand to go to their charity that sends sick kids to swim with dolphins. (What is it with sick kids and dolphins? They're proper obsessed with them, aren't they? If I ever find myself thinking about dolphins a lot I'm getting myself down to Dr. Gupta's right away.)

Barney Draper says that he's had folks of every color and creed enjoying his nativity: white, black, beige, and green. "EVERYBODY, so the council can stick their Christmas ban right up their 'arris!"

Some people have been enjoying the nativity a bit too much, mind. The baby Jesus went missing for twenty-four hours on Saturday night after a drunk bloke nicked him on the way home from Goodmayes Social. He brought him back though. The bloke said he was so hammered he felt proper sorry for baby Jesus sitting there freezing with his frankincense and myrrh so he took him home for some of his lamb shish kebab.

Anyway, I'm proper excited tonight as we're going on our Christmas trip to London to see *King Lear* tomorrow! Carrie says the dress code is "Dress to Impress with a nod toward Academia."

Balls to that, I'm wearing my jeans, my pink hoodie, and my gold.

THURSDAY 18TH DECEMBER

Oh God. Oh no. no. no. NO NO NO.

I feel properly awful today. Awful, terrible, nasty — but at the same time, a bit amazing. Yesterday all of us Sixth Formers went to London and it turned into one of the most brilliant days of my whole life ever. Even better than the day my family went on *Fast-Track Family Feud* on ITV2 and even better than the day Wesley first came round my house and asked me out and better than the day I got my GCSEs and realized I wasn't thick. Better than all of that.

I ain't eaten one single thing today and I never even went to school. I just lay under the duvet in my room thinking and thinking and praying and I ain't even religious or nothing but the one thing Sonia Cathcart always says is that if you ask Jesus Christ Our Savior for his divine guidance then suddenly he'll spring up like a genie out a bottle or something and help you out. Well I've been under here for eight hours asking him to sort this mess out for me and he ain't helped me at all. All I know is I'm well confused and I feel like a right slapper.

Basically, me, Carrie, Sean, Uma, Saf, Joshua, Ms. Bracket, and loads of other folks went through on the train and the tube to London yesterday at about 3PM. It was snowy and quite dark when we came up from the tube station and there was a brass band playing on Charing Cross Road and zillions of Christmas shoppers everywhere and tourists and office workers and commuters and all the shop windows had Christmas displays and everywhere you looked there were tipsy people staggering out of Christmas office parties and bus drivers wearing flashing antlers and Santa Clauses on every corner collecting charity money and traffic jams and noise. We were all having such a giggle, me and Carrie and everyone. I just felt proper Christmassy and dizzy and alive.

I always want to come to London but Wesley never wants to come. Wesley can't see the point. Wesley says it's smelly and full of freaks. And I used to think that too for a long time, especially when Cava-Sue used to go on about it. But now I don't because the thing is when you get to London and you stand on Waterloo Bridge over the Thames and look both ways along the river and there's Big Ben and the London Eye and the Houses of Parliament and St. Paul's Cathedral and loads of other amazing buildings and lasers and lights and the river is flowing beneath you, well, it is properly the most beautiful thing EVER.

And it really changes how you feel about life 'cos suddenly you're part of this one amazing, big universe and you feel like exciting stuff can happen and you're not just stuck in Goodmayes doing school stuff and you feel properly in awe of the world and what can go on here and it changes how you feel about everything FOREVER. Wesley can never see that about London. I wish I could bring Wesley to that bridge and show him, but he would never want to come.

Me and Carrie and Saf and Josh and Uma and Sean stood on Waterloo Bridge and stared at the view for a while and took photos of each other and Josh pointed out mental stuff no one noticed before like weird faces on buildings that he called gargoyles and statues up on roofs. Then Sean took a group picture of us all for our MySpace and Josh put his arm round me and touched my shoulder and it felt really good.

Then Sean said, "Hang on, that's a nice picture, Shiz, just you and Josh together?" and we both wrapped our arms round each other's waists and pretended to cuddle which was just a joke but it felt amazing and I KNOW I should have been thinking, "What would my Wesley say if he saw me pretend-cuddling?" But the fact is I wasn't thinking about my Wesley. He wasn't in my mind at all.

So we went to see *King Lear* performed by folks from the Royal Shakespeare Company and it was TOTALLY BRILLIANT, 'cos fair enough, it's one thing reading it out in class, but when you see all these people really being Cordelia and Goneril and King Lear then it proper brings it to life and you get well caught up in it. And when King Lear was cast out into the storm I could feel myself starting to cry 'cos I started thinking about Nan and how awful it would be if we all turned on her and made her homeless and by the time the play was over — THREE HOURS LATER — I was properly buzzing. And by this point it was 10 o'clock and Ms. Bracket started to "seriously recommend" that we all got the tube home which was her trying to force us but she didn't have no power to and the thing was Joshua had sorted out free guest list passes at this club called Forever Friends off Trafalgar Square. So Carrie says, "Oh come on, Shiz, we can get a night bus home! It'll be good!" and I should have said no but I didn't, I said yes 'cos I knew Josh wanted me to go 'cos he kept looking at me proper intense. Well anyway, Forever Friends was bloody amazing and it was packed out and the DJ was playing bits of hip-hop and bits of random silly party stuff and '70s disco and I don't know what quite happened in there but I think I lost a bit of my mind 'cos suddenly we were all dancing up on the stage, me and Saf and Sean and Josh and Uma and Carrie and we were so happy and we were laughing and hugging each other and talking total nonsense about life and how much we all loved each other and how we'd all be friends forever just like the club was called Forever Friends and at one point I was dancing with Josh and he was holding me round the waist and looking right in my eyes and suddenly I realized I just wanted to snog him, no, SNOG HIS FACE OFF, but I didn't 'cos I knew that was well wrong.

But then the club lights went on and we all got turfed out and everyone in the club spilled out into the streets and everybody was on a proper Christmas high and everyone started flooding into Trafalgar Square and we all followed, then people started getting into the fountains and splashing about and me and Josh climbed up on one of the bases of the sculpted lions and we sat together and watched Carrie and Saf and Sean running about in the fountains. Then Josh got hold of my hand suddenly and kissed it and he said, "So can I have my Christmas snog?" and I was so carried away with the moment that I snogged him and it felt totally bloody amazing and squelchy and hot and just gagggggggggggh! (And that ain't even a word!!!) And the second he stopped snogging me I suddenly remembered Wesley Barrington Bains II and I felt bad.

"What's up?" Josh said.

"I've got a boyfriend," I said. "I shouldn't be doing this."

"Oh c'mon, Shiraz," said Josh. "I've been after you for ages. You feel the same."

"No. I don't. It's not like that," I said, but I sounded proper confused. "I don't know what to do!"

"Well, I know what you've gotta do," he said. "You've got to bin that Wesley guy and be with me. I want you." Then he kissed me again, for longer that time.

Then we rounded everyone up and we all got the night bus home together and I came straight in the house and got straight into this bed and started worrying and so far Jesus Christ Our Savior has come up with no guidance whatsoever.

Maybe it's because I am GOING TO HELL.

SUNDAY 21ST DECEMBER

This has been the hardest four days of my whole life EVER. So much for Jesus Christ Our Savior. I suppose some messes you've just got to sort out on your own. I am TRYING MY BEST to ignore Joshua but he texts me every day. Proper naughty texts that I have to DELETE right away. About stuff he'd like to do with me.

Stuff I've never done before and wasn't planning on doing for a while yet. It is driving me mental. I was in a right state getting everyone's Christmas pressies today. I've left it far too late.

My nan has ended up with some extra-strong denture fix glue and my brother got a calendar called "Naughty Babes" which I've now looked through properly and realize is not suitable for a fifteen-year-old at all 'cos by April the "babes" have totally given up wearing knickers or even sitting upright with their knees shut altogether. I got Wesley some antifreeze and a new ice-scraper. I'm just too busy these days for Christmas pressies. I hope they all understand.

THURSDAY 25TH DECEMBER, CHRISTMAS DAY

10PM — I don't know if what happened today really happened. I'm a bit confused. I'm going to write it all down and see if it makes more sense.

So today was Christmas Day which is always one of the best days of the whole year in our house 'cos we sort of do the same stuff every single year like a little pattern. We pull Christmas crackers and we open a tin of Quality Street chocolates and me and Cava-Sue argue over the green triangles and we all get a bit tipsy on Bucks Fizz and we eat a massive meal of turkey and vegetables that makes you feel proper farty.

Nan comes round and she always gets new Christmas fluffy slippers and she always falls asleep after dinner with her gob open and we always make jokes about her looking like the Dartford Tunnel. About twenty minutes after Christmas dinner finishes Mum starts clattering about in the kitchen then produces an extra large lattice-top pork pie and two hundred ham sandwiches and a bread pudding then gets the hump when no one will "pull their weight" and eat any.

We always wear stupid paper hats all day and Dad always tries to claim he saw Santa when he was up at 5AM cooking the turkey and Mum always wears a smart outfit all day and lipstick that gradually slides down her face. And at night we sit down and watch a movie on BBC1 but everyone always talks all the way through it and the phone keeps ringing with mad relatives who only call up once a year to say Happy Christmas and my mum talks to them all using her posh phone voice and we all giggle and eat After Eight mints and feel happy but a bit sick.

This year was totally the same as always, but different too.

For a start Nan brought Clement with her, who was in a proper happy mood and he turned up in a Santa hat with a big bottle of rum. So right away Dad and Clement started having a "wee nip just to test its consistency" and being proper silly and not concentrating on the brussels sprouts which was their job.

Everyone — Cava-Sue, Lewis, Mum, Murphy, Nan, they were laughing and joking and I thought I was too but I can't have been 'cos folks kept asking me "What's wrong with your mush?" and telling me, "Cheer up, it might never happen!" When of course I wanted to shout "IT HAS HAPPENED! I'VE CHEATED ON WESLEY BARRINGTON BAINS II WITH JOSHUA FALLOW AND I THINK I'VE FALLEN IN LOVE!!!"

Eventually Wesley turned up wearing his new navy Ralph Lauren Christmas sweatshirt from his mum. He was holding a big box which was all fancy-wrapped like Sonia Cathcart had been at it giving it the full yee-hah with some glitter and tinsel bows. The moment Wesley stepped in the house everyone cheered then started making funny comments about the big fancy present he was holding saying, "'Ere, Wesley, don't get too excited about your gift from Shiraz! 'Cos we've all had ours. Flipping heck! No expense spared, mate!"

And this was when I started to realize I'd PROPER MESSED UP with Wesley's present. 'Cos Wesley loves Christmas and Wesley loves giving presents and here he is with a big sparkly box of something amazing and here's me with a can of antifreeze. And now I see that in no way is this going to be funny, like it was when Cava-Sue opened her Swiss Army Knife.

I thought we could do with some privacy so we went to my room. Wesley sat on the bed and looked at me and it was horrible 'cos it was like he KNEW about Josh but he couldn't have, it was just me being paranoid. Then he passed me his present which I unwrapped, and it was something proper amazing. It was this well expensive desk lamp called an "anglepoise" like proper writers have. It was from that posh shop that Carrie always goes on about called Habitat.

"Do you like it?" Wesley said.

"I love it," I said, feeling even more terrible now. "When did you get it?!"

"Oh, I drove to London for it last week when you were at Mr. Yolk," he said.

"You went all the way to London?!" I said.

112

"Yeah." He smiled. "Proper nightmare that place is. Well smelly."

It was when I gave him the antifreeze that things started going properly tits up. Wesley started saying having no time is no excuse at Christmas 'cos everyone is busy. How I never have no time for him anymore. How ever since I started Sixth Form it's like I'm a different person and he don't know if he can put up with the new me.

So I said, "Oh bloody BUGGER OFF then, Wesley. 'Cos this is me now and I'm going to keep on being me and I AIN'T BLOODY CHANGING!"

Wesley picked up his antifreeze and his new scraper and his car keys and said, "Well, that's that then, Shiraz, innit. See ya around." Then he gave me a kiss on the forehead and walked down the stairs, out the door, and drove off.

I sat on the edge of my bed for a bit and felt well upset and sick and relieved all at the same time. Then I went downstairs into the kitchen where Nan and Clement were dancing together by the sink to a song by Shakin' Stevens on Radio Essex. They had their hands around each other's waists, looking into each other's eyes like they were a bit in love with each other. When I walked in they both stopped.

So, reading this through all again from the top, it seems that me and Wesley Barrington Bains II are over. And my Nan is getting it on with Clement.

That Jesus Christ is quite obviously celebrating his birthday by having a right old giggle at my expense.

FRIDAY 26TH DECEMBER

Latanoyatiqua Marshall-Dinsdale was born today at 4AM. She was 7lb. 2oz. Kezia had her at home in her mum's living room with Kezia's mum and sisters all helping out and holding her ankles. Kezia says it was proper painful. Like going to the loo, then realizing you had to try and push out a big watermelon one millimeter at a time but for nine whole hours.

Kezia's baby is well nice though. She's a lovely, brown, plump lump with long eyelashes. Me and Carrie and Uma went round to see her tonight. Carrie was too scared to hold her but I wasn't. I tucked her into my chest and for some reason my stomach went all funny and I wanted to cry.

I told Kezia that me and Wesley had split up. Kezia says that I'm better off without a bloke, 'cos they all let you down in the end just like her Luther did. Carrie says to Kezia that I've no place to moan 'cos I'll soon be upgrading Wesley for "something a lot better." I know she means Joshua Fallow.

Carrie is hassling me and Uma to go to Joshua's New Year's Eve party at his house next week but I'm not too sure. You should see some of the texts he's been sending me. Proper rude they are. It's all he ever thinks about. Not that I don't think about rude things too sometimes. Saying that, Kezia's story about the watermelon has put me off a bit. Nothing's worth that trouble.

SATURDAY 27TH DECEMBER

Sat 27 Dec 5:06
FROM: JOSHUA
HI SHIZ — PRTY AT MINE
ON NEW YRS EVE.
U R COMIN ARENT U?
JUST SAY YES.
I'LL MAKE IT
WORTH YOUR WHILE.
LET'S START
NEW YEAR WITH A
BANG. ADDRESS: 37
VERENCE ROAD. 9PM.
XXXXX:OXXXXXXXXX

Sat 27 Dec 5:46
FROM: SHIRAZ
HI JOSH — NT SURE
BOUT PARTY. HEAD
BIT MIXED UP NOW.
MAY JUST HAVE A
QUIET ONE. CHEERS
FOR INVITE. SHIZZA

Sat 27 Dec 8:07
FROM: JOSHUA
SHUT UP AND GET YOUR
FINE BOOTY OVER TO MY
HOUSE N.Y.E. OR ELSE.
WANT TO SEE
YOUR EYES AND YOUR
SMILE AND YOUR NICE
BIG PAIR OF . . .

Sat 27 Dec 8:09
FROM: JOSHUA
. . . HOOP EARRINGS!
(SOZ FOR DELAY, GOT
DISTRACTED THINKING
BOUT THAT SNOG WE HAD.)
MMMMMMMMMMMMM.

Sat 27 Dec 9:19
FROM: SHIRAZ
STOP IT! STOP BENDING
MY HEAD. YOU ARE A
PROPER LIBERTY
JOSHUA EZRA FALLOW!
GET OUT OF MY BRAIN.

Sat 27 Dec 10:15
FROM: JOSHUA
HA, GOT YOU
THINKING THO.
SO YOU'LL COME
TO THE PARTY? IT'LL
BE GOOD. I PROMISE.
JUST COME. X

Sat 27 Dec 11:12
FROM: JOSHUA
SHIRAZ BAILEY WOOD!
R U THERE???
R U COMING????

Sat 27 Dec 11:45
FROM: SHIRAZ
OK X

JANUARY

THURSDAY 1ST JANUARY

I was planning to blow off Josh's party yesterday and stay in with my folks instead. Fact is I was feeling proper odd what with everyone on TV bloody going on and on about New Year's Eve and "fresh starts" and "taking stock of the last twelve months" and here's me just split with this bloke who properly loved me but now reckons I'm well up myself and I miss him like mad but I don't want to get back with him 'cos all he chats about is Vauxhall Novas and his plumbing NVQ and I've met this other boy who is well buff with pointy cheekbones who actually reads books and thinks about life.

"So what you up to this evening? Out gallivanting?" my mother says at about 5 o'clock and I sighs and goes, "Nah, I'm going to stay in with you lot I reckon." And my mother says "Oh, well we are very honored I'm sure, but you'll have a bleeding job of it 'cos me and your father are going to a Tom Jones tribute act at Goodmayes Social. Five quid a ticket and you get your buffet for that too! Good, eh?" So I goes, "You're what!? You're going out? You ALWAYS stay in on New Year's Eve!" and Mum says, "Yeah, and I always have to sit here looking at your sour face 'cos you want to be out partying! Well you're seventeen now so I thought you'd be off out and staying at Carrie Draper's so I made plans! Or should I have cleared it with Her Royal Highness first?"

I just gave her my stroppiest WHATEVER look.

"'Ere, and by the way," she says, "Cava-Sue and Lewis and Murphy are all at parties too, so if you are staying in will you make sure Dick Clark's New Year's Rockin' Eve with Ryan Seacrest records on the DVR for Cava-Sue and will you let the dog out for a jimmy-widdle at 11PM 'cos you know she likes one just before bed, after she's had her Pringles?"

At that point I decided I was off to Josh's party. But I was well late getting ready by this time, so I ran around the house like a mental, rounding up my best jeans, top, and hoodie from various laundry baskets and sticking them in the washing machine and putting them on the radiators to get them dried fast, which ended up in another stand-up with my mother who could sniff a radiator being put on in Australia I reckon. Mum then starts tracking me around the house moaning about heating bills and about me not giving her no money toward stuff now I'm in Sixth Form and basically doing my head in by going on and on like that for about forty-five minutes while I just ignored her and wished she had a bloody mute button.

So I walked down Thundersley Road and knocked for Uma, who looked proper amazing in skin-tight black trousers and a black off-the-shoulder top and big hoops and fake tan, 'cos she'd had a big win on the Poker and had been treating herself down at New Look. I waited while she fed Zeus then we set off for Josh's house.

Josh lives over on the far side of Goodmayes on this posh street called Verence Road which is up near the hospital. It's all really big old-fashioned-looking terraced houses up there with quite spooky trees along the pavements. My mother always says a lot of the doctors and the psychiatrists from the hospital live round there and I'm sure Cava-Sue once said one of her lecturers from her AS-Level Theater Studies lived down Verence Road too. It felt well different there to Thundersley Road 'cos no one had decorations on the front of their houses at all and everyone seemed well obsessed with recycling boxes and the only houses that had rubbish or weeds in their front gardens looked like they were being gutted by builders to be completely done up and a few of the houses had scaffolding up the front like they were making the lofts bigger, as if the houses weren't flipping big enough already.

We walked up to number 37, which had a big black door and big bay window like my mum always gets excited about on them "do your house up" shows she watches. "Ooh I love them big Victorian bays!" she always says, "Just like my granny used to have over in Stockwell when I was a little girl!"

I was thinking about that as we rang the doorbell and waited. It seemed like there was a proper noisy party going on.

Suddenly the door flings opens and there's this lady who's about fifty standing there in a long black dress with brown hair all piled up on the top her head sort of willy-nilly holding a glass of red wine. She looks at us and shouts, "Youngs or olds?" and we go "Eh?" and she goes "Which party do you want? Ancient people downstairs, hip young gunslingers up in the loft!"

"Erm, Joshua, innit?" said Uma.

"Of course," howled the woman who had a bit of mentalist laugh to be honest. "Up the stairs, keep on going, up two flights.

Oh, and will you tell him if anyone is smoking up there to keep the skylight ajar as I've just had the upstairs painted and I don't want it smoked out."

"Mmmmokthankyou," we said.

We walked past her and down the hall where loads of grown-ups were standing about drinking wine and yakking. Snow Patrol was blaring out of the living room and I'm sure I could smell hash smoke floating out of the kitchen. The blokes were wearing jeans and suit jackets and some had beards and the women looked a bit like teachers and they all seemed to have extra-loud voices and one woman was moaning about how some documentary she'd just finished assistant-producing had changed air dates TWICE and she'd just fired off a stinking e-mail to the BBC and another woman was telling everyone that she'd reduced her carbon footprint by ninety percent in six months. Me and Uma got down the hallway as fast as we could then practically ran up the stairs.

Joshua actually has his own floor of the house. HIS OWN FLOOR!!! You know how my room is so small that I have to get out of bed and go onto the landing and reverse back in again if I want to turn over in bed? Well Joshua don't have this problem as he has his own bloody massive bedroom in the attic with room for a double bed, a sofa, and his own bloody en suite bathroom!!!

When we got up to Joshua's room there was about thirty-five kids up there from Mayflower and Regis Hill Boys and Waltham-stow Grange and a few girls from North West London who Josh said were his sort-of cousins and everyone was laughing and chatting and screaming and shouting and jumping on the bed and

drinking cider and hanging out of the skylight and smoking cig-
arettes and this weird lad called Nozz kept showing everyone he
could do backflips and everyone was fighting over the stereo trying to plug in their iPods and playing hip-hop and Dubstep and
R&B. It was the most wicked party I've EVER seen in real life.

Then Carrie showed up with Saf and Sean and by this point
everyone was dancing or falling about or they were on their
phones calling other folks to tell them about Josh's party or taking photos of each other to send to other kids to prove what a
legendary party it was. And the hours started to really fly by then
because everything got really messy and at one point I was so
happy and dizzy I thought I was on a different planet, in fact I
don't even remember it turning midnight at all. And from the
moment me and Josh hooked up we just had such a proper laugh
with each other and I totally forgot about the split-up with Wesley
'cos me and Josh were flirting and chatting then cuddling then
snogging then REALLY REALLY snogging each other and everyone who saw us was saying what a well cute couple we were and
Joshua didn't argue with that he just held me even closer and
told everyone I was his now. And I felt properly like I was in love
although I knew it must just be my head playing tricks and jum-
bling stuff up.

And somehow when I didn't even notice, it started getting
light and everyone was beginning to get taxis and me and Josh
ended up curled up on the floor with a blanket over us watching
some mad film on DVD with subtitles and just chatting total rubbish about proper randomness like books and music and what
superhero power we'd both like to have for one day and all sorts

of crap and it just felt totally amazing with Josh there wrapped around me under the blanket talking to me proper intensely about life and sometimes biting and kissing my neck. And we stayed there for ages doing stuff and eventually passed out and when I woke up it was midday and there was no one else there but me and Josh lying on a floor surrounded by bottles and party poppers.

I grabbed all my stuff and kissed his snoring face and ran off home and quickly got in the shower and stood there for ages thinking.

I feel like I'll never be the same person ever again.

SATURDAY 3RD JANUARY

Me and Joshua are going out. I'm Joshua's girlfriend! Me? JOSHUA FALLOW? He's like the buffest boy in Mayflower and he wants to go out with me! ME! He fancies me! He says he can't stop thinking about me and I can't stop thinking about him either. I feel sick all the time. I just want to be with him every minute. Like right now when I'm lying in bed here all I want to do is run out of the door and run to his house on Verence Road and see him and smell him and kiss him and wrap my arms and legs round him. I think I'm going mad. I want to tell everyone in the whole world. I want to get on the top deck of the number 56 bus and ride round and round Ilford shouting it at passersby.

But we're going to try and keep it quietish for a bit 'cos I don't want Wesley to know. He's going to think I'm a right hoochie. I hope he's not too upset.

THURSDAY 8TH JANUARY

I went over to Joshua's after school tonight. We were planning on doing some reading for English 'cos it was back to school this week, but it's proper difficult studying when you're on your own with Joshua in his room 'cos he is so choong that it is well distracting. I keep finding little bits of him I ain't never noticed or kissed before. I like the bits behind his ears and the end of his nose.

I met Joshua's mum properly today. She didn't seem to remember me from New Year's Eve. I only met her for five minutes in the kitchen tonight and I said hello and smiled at her but she just sort of looked at me a bit funny. She stared at my hoop earrings and my hoodie and my scrunchie and my rings like she'd never seen anything like it before, then Josh told her I was called Shiraz and she said, "How lovely." Then she said, "Well, your friend will need to go now because we're sitting down for supper as soon as Dad's finished speaking to L.A."

I came home and my mother was giving Penny a bath in the kitchen sink and my dad was clipping his toenails in front of the TV and Murphy was moaning 'cos the clippings kept nearly landing in his Coco Pops. I just spoke to Josh on the phone and he was asking when he can come to my house. I just laughed and said when hell freezes over mate.

MONDAY 12TH JANUARY

Mayflower was proper stressful today. Everyone's going on about studying now because it counts toward the final AS grade. EVERYONE: Saf, Sean, Sonia, Manpreet, Tonita, Nabila, even my Josh. They're all PROPER OBSESSED with getting good home-work grades and getting good AS grades 'cos everyone reckons if you get good AS grades then you can get good A2 levels next year and then if you get good predicted A2 grades and have good hobbies and stuff for your uni application forms then you can go to a good uni. Then if you go to a good uni you can get a good job and if you got a good job you can buy a big house and if you work hard every day after that you can get an even better job and . . . and . . . bloody hell I'm knackered just listening to everyone.

That's one good thing about knocking about with Carrie. She ain't like everyone else. Carrie didn't show up until noon today and when Mr. Douglas started nagging her about missing Busi-ness Studies class she just tutted and said she'd done a Fake Bake deep-bronze tan last night and it was still sticky so she couldn't get her thong on over her lady-garden. Mr. Douglas's face went so RED. I love Carrie Draper. She is bare jokes. I can't see Bar-ney's business lasting long with her in charge, mind you.

THURSDAY 15TH JANUARY

Lewis's mother in Benidorm has agreed to give Cava-Sue and Lewis a loan to go traveling!!! They are leaving for Vietnam in two weeks! That's two less people using the bathroom in the morning. Some mornings I don't even get a shower before school! I just have to spray more deodorant on and hope for the best. I asked Mum if I can have Cava-Sue's room and we can put in another bathroom. My mother just tutted and said, "A bathroom?!! Ha! Well I think we said goodbye to another bathroom the moment you gave poor Wesley the plumber the boot! Oh, and I saw him today outside Sears, by the way. He looked like death warmed up! You broke that one's heart you did!"

I felt like crap when she said that. I'm guessing Wes has seen the photos on everyone's MySpace of Joshua's party. The ones where I'm snogging Josh.

Then Mum says, "So what does this new one of yours want to be then?" And I went red when she said that, 'cos I didn't think she knew about Joshua, then I remembered that me, Murphy, and Cava-Sue all trade little bits of info to Mum in return for favors so I mumbled a bit and said, "'Erm I dunno what Joshua wants to be, a politician I think." And my mother laughed and said, "Well if he's got two faces and a slithering tail he'll be fine."

I tried calling Josh for a chat to cheer myself up, but his phone went straight to voicemail.

WEDNESDAY 21ST JANUARY

I was down at Uma's tonight. There was a time when I'd never have hung out round there, 'cos Uma used to be a proper loon, but she's a bit different now. I wish other people could see it. Uma don't smoke weed anymore so she's not as paranoid. She never even sees Tiffany or Ashleen who she used to go drinking with in the park.

It's not like Uma's suddenly an angel or nothing. I just reckon her stepdad going to jail and her mum leaving her with Clinton just gave her a big wake-up call. My mum still don't trust Uma though. She never will.

"How is she surviving for money? That's what I wonder!" my mother keeps saying. "Mugging grannies and dealing drugs, I reckon! Or much worse! And that devil dog of hers wants to be put down too."

Me and Uma never mugged any grannies tonight. We shared a box of cookies and talked about *King Lear*.

SUNDAY 25TH JANUARY

WEIRD DAY. Josh never called me last night like he said he would 'cos we sort of half said we'd maybe go to the AMC Loews, but I texted at 5PM to check and he never texted me back and then his phone was turned off. He's not like Wesley when it comes to plans. He's sort of unpredictable. But I'm fine with that though 'cos at least I've got lots of space. Anyway Josh rang me this morning and said, "Sorry, babycakes, I ended up going out with my sort-of cousins in North London." And I said "No worries, that's fine." Because it totally was.

"Come over and bring your *King Lear* notes!" he said, so I jumped in the shower right away and made myself look all glam and bling and got there as soon as I could 'cos I'd proper missed him. So I got to Josh's house and rang the doorbell and he answers the door and said, "Come down into the kitchen for a bit, me and Mum are in there."

So I went into the kitchen and Mrs. Fallow was sitting at the table, looking at the magazine from the *Observer* newspaper and drinking coffee and eating a bar of expensive looking dark chocolate. Weird opera music was playing on a little stereo on the counter and a big black cat called Marx was sitting on the Sports Section, washing his bum.

To be honest, I didn't feel very welcome in there, 'cos when Mrs. Fallow saw me she reckoned she'd never met me before again. Then eventually she remembered she had and then she said, "Remind me. You're Joshua's friend from where precisely?" doing a scan of my hoodie and hoops just like last time.

And I felt like saying, "I'm not his *friend*. I'm his *girlfriend*!" But it didn't seem the right thing to do. Then she stood up and opened the door of this weird iron cupboard thing that looked like an oven but can't have been.

"Mayflower Academy," I said, not knowing whether to sit down or stand up and what the weird oven-cupboard thing was.

So I said, "What is that?" and she just looked at me with this kind of smile that wasn't a proper smile and said, "It's an Aga." I just nodded like I knew what that was.

Then Josh got a plate of banana bread and granola bars and some chips and pomegranate juice for us both and we went upstairs and snogged loads and lay about on his sofa. I couldn't stay long though 'cos I was going down to bingo with Nan tonight at Chadwell Heath.

As I was leaving Josh's house I thought I'd pop down into the kitchen and say a quick goodbye to Mrs. Fallow then she might remember me next time, but as I got halfway down the hall I could hear her on the phone with someone.

"Oh I know," she was laughing. "I'm terrible, I know! I KNOW! I'll go to hell . . . Ha ha ha! The thing is it was Josh's father's idea to send him to Mayflower Academy. 'Oooh it's a Center of Excellence now,' he said! 'Think of the cash we'll save on school fees,' he said! 'It'll make Joshy more streetwise,' he said!"

I should have just walked away and stopped earwigging then, but I stayed a bit longer and then Mrs. Fallow laughed her nutty laugh again and said, "Oh God, I know, Jocasta, I'm just being wicked. It's just, for the love of god, I make my donation to Christian Aid! I'm sponsoring a little African girl in Burkina Faso! I don't see why I've got to feed the chavs from the local projects too. Ha ha ha!"

I felt proper sick then so I ran out of the door and ran home. I'm sure she wasn't talking about me. I'm just being a bit paranoid, aren't I?

She never meant me.

FEBRUARY

MONDAY 2ND FEBRUARY

Cava-Sue and Lewis left for Vietnam today. It's weird 'cos I'm missing Cava-Sue already and only two days ago I was thinking what a right pain in the ass she was, wiffling on about the awful human rights violations of the Vietnamese people and how some poor peasant folks in Nam Pam Lang have no access to information and I was sitting there thinking, "Flaming hell, they're not going to know what's hit them when you get there with your big clacking gob."

Then suddenly, her and Lewis have packed their backpacks and gone. All the talking about it is finally over. Cava-Sue has gone off following her dream. It's really made me think about my dream. I still don't really know what it is.

We had a little going-away party for Cava-Sue and Lewis in our house yesterday and because everyone had been giving me proper earache about inviting Joshua (including Joshua himself) I let him come over. To be honest, I was proper paranoid about asking Josh to my house 'cos ever since I heard his mum say that nasty thing which I don't even know for sure was about me, well it makes my face go proper hot.

I haven't been wearing my gold hoops at all recently. Or my charm bracelet. And I even feel a bit weird in my hoodie 'cos I keep thinking, "Does this make me look like a chav? Am I a chav?

Am I? No, I ain't a chav! Chavs are people like those little hoodrats who hang round the park and those rudes who jack folks's phones outside Ilford station! I'm not like that! Am I?"

But then I think what I might look like to a woman who has friends called Jocasta, who has enough money to have a stupid hot cupboard instead of an oven and sponsor kids in Burkina Faso and give her son his own bathroom and suddenly I feel all terrible and a bit, well . . . a bit like a chav.

So I bring Joshua back to my house on Thundersley Road and I've spent months being proper vague about where it is 'cos I didn't want him to just show up, but now here we both are walking down the road together and I'm totally noticing all the stuff I never even noticed before, like the broken sidewalk and the white dog poos and the road sign with grafitti willies on it and the way Bert at number 89 hangs his underpants up on a line in his garden and how everyone has Staffy dogs. Then we walk past Uma's house with the fridge in the garden and Joshua snorts and says, "I suppose that saves space in the house!" And I cringe a bit and say, "That's Uma's house." And Joshua goes, "Oh, that makes sense."

In our house, my mum, my dad, Murphy, Clement, and Nan were all there laughing and talking and eating a buffet from Tyson's that Mum had just bought and shoved out on plates. And they're all drinking Peach Lambrella wine and little stubby bottles of German beer and listening to Dad's Chas 'n' Dave record and being silly and noisy. And it's weird 'cos now I'm noticing stuff like the wear on the hall carpet and the chipped paint and the way our house smells a little bit of the dog and the way there's framed photos of us all everywhere and how no one is using a plate for the buffet and how everyone is shouting and not listening to each other's answers and how bloody small the house is. And to be honest I think Joshua is pretty stunned by everything 'cos he hardly says a word and at one point when my nan got up and started singing I could swear he was trying not to stop himself smirking.

My nan asked Josh what he was studying and he said English, Politics, Geography, and Critical Theory and everyone went, "Wooooooh! Clever clogs!" like it was something amazing, then Nan asked him what he wanted to be and he said, "Well I'll be off to Oxford University next to study Diplomacy and International Relations I hope. If they'll have me." And no one said nothing to that 'cos I think they were too gobsmacked.

I don't know if Joshua enjoyed the party. My mum said afterward he never ate none of the buffet. I said, well, Joshua's mum never lets him eat nothing with additives or non-organic so he probably didn't reckon his delicate stomach would stand the fried cheese or the reconstituted seafood ring. My mum said something quite rude then about shoving the fried cheese where the sun don't shine for all she cares, but I think she was quite tipsy and emotional.

I miss Cava-Sue. I hope she stays in touch.

THURSDAY 5TH FEBRUARY

I had a bit of a funny thing happen today. We'd got the marks back for our English coursework — well, most of us, not Carrie, 'cos she was "ill" again — and everyone was in the common room feeling pretty happy 'cos we'd all done fairly well. So, everyone was chatting about grades and Manpreet had got an A and Josh had got an A and I'd got a B and Sonia had got an A and Uma had got a C and everyone was just chatting away about what that meant and what grades this might mean for the future and about jobs in offices and getting a smart suit for uni interviews and suddenly I started feeling really weird 'cos I was the only one not talking and I realized I was the only one who didn't really care.

I never admitted it to anyone but I suddenly realized I don't care about going to uni. I suddenly realized the thought of carrying on studying as hard as this for loads more years was making me feel as trapped as that time I was parked around the back of Bishop Fledding Industrial Estate looking at a pile of rubble that Wesley wanted me to live in with him forever.

I don't want to feel trapped like this. I want to feel like I did when I stood on Waterloo Bridge in London among all the crowds and the traffic and the gargoyles and statues when I looked along the river and felt properly blown away and excited and free and like anything was possible. I think I'm due for my period. I'll feel better tomorrow.

FRIDAY 13TH FEBRUARY

No word from Cava-Sue. I hope she's OK. There's a small chance she's been captured by a rare mountain cannibal tribe who've tried to barbecue her head to shut her up from telling them interesting facts about themselves.

I'm a bit narked today 'cos I was just speaking to Carrie and she says Saf is taking her to Le Galle restaurant in Romford tomorrow night for a three-course Valentine's dinner. Then I spoke to my nan and she reckons Clement is cooking her dinner round at his place, then I come home and our Murphy is stealing a red felt pen from my room to write a card to some girl he's seeing and he's covering it with hearts and kisses like he is proper in love. (Murphy! In love?? With a girl called Rema in Year Nine. Not a PS2 game. Mental.)

So I ask my Joshua what he was getting me for Valentine's Day today and he laughs at me like I am a weirdo and says, "Ha! You're kidding, aren't you? Don't tell me you buy into that capitalist conspiracy? It was invented by a card shop to make money. What do you want, one of those big tacky teddy bears with I WUV YOU on it too! Ha ha ha ha!" So I said, "No, course I don't, but, well, but . . ."

And I didn't have no answer 'cos Josh has a way of making you feel really small which he must have learned off his mum. So I said, "Well I just want to feel like you CARE!" and Josh says "Oh, OK, OK, Shiraz. Look I didn't want to spoil the surprise but I've actually booked one of them planes to fly past Thundersley Road dragging a banner. I'll just run along now and call air traffic control and see if it's on its way."

And I said "You haven't???!!!" And he said, "No, of course I haven't, you silly mare! You know how much I'm into you, what MORE do you want?"

I'm sure he must be kidding me. 'Cos everyone likes Valentines Day really, don't they?

SATURDAY 14TH FEBRUARY

MENTAL NEWS OF THE YEAR ALERT: my nan is getting married to Clement! She is seventy-three and he is seventy-eight but Nan says that finding him makes her feel seventeen again, so they're going to get hitched to show the world they're in love. Nan says he cooked her a chicken round at his place tonight and she was helping with the spuds, then when she turned round at one point she found him down on one knee by the sink and she thought, "Oh Christ Almighty, he's having a stroke!" but then she noticed he was holding a ring in a ring box. They've set a date for July!

I wasn't so lucky today. It seems my Josh meant that thing about the "capitalist conspiracy." I spent tonight sitting indoors with my mum and dad.

Josh said there was no way he was booking any restaurant tonight 'cos it would be full of mushy couples. Josh said he'd rather spend the night in Fat Freddy's Foodstop in Romford with all the superchavs and that's saying something. "There's nothing wrong with Fat Freddy's Foodstop!!!" I wanted to yell, but I didn't want him to know I'd ever been.

SUNDAY 15TH FEBRUARY

I was lying in bed this morning sort of sulking a bit about Joshua, when my dad knocked on my door and shouted, "Woo-hoo! Shiraz Bailey Wood. There's been a special delivery!" And suddenly everything felt better 'cos I knew Joshua had been joking all along and he'd bought me a pressie.

So I went downstairs in my pajamas, and sitting on the floor in the living room was a massive red envelope about a meter high. A massive soggy envelope. With SHIRAZ BAILEY WOOD written on the front in magic marker, but the letters had all ran 'cos the envelope was damp from being outside. When I looked closer there was a bug crawling up the front.

"Where did this come from?" I said, 'cos right away I knew this wasn't from Josh.

"It was sitting on the front doorstep just now," said my dad. "Someone must have brought it round in the night. It's a bit wet, look."

"Did you see them?" I said.

"No, it must have been really late," said Dad. "Oh, and they left this too."

Dad passed me a tube wrapped in shiny paper. Inside was a tube of candy Smarties. But when I looked at it closely it wasn't any old tube of Smarties. It was all blue Smarties. Somebody had bought lots and lots of tubes of Smarties and fished out all the blue ones and put them all into one tube so I could have lots and lots of my favorite blue ones. Then they'd come in the middle of the night in the rain with a big card and dropped them off. The card didn't say who it was from. It just said, "For Shiraz, the most beautiful girl in Goodmayes xxxx."

Me and Dad never said to each other but we both knew who it was from. It was from someone who cared.

MONDAY 23RD FEBRUARY

It's funny 'cos I was just thinking today about that "Increase the Peace" campaign and thinking, y'know maybe it was a big waste of time and maybe Josh was right, folks did do it just to put something good on their uni application forms after all. Because it's been five months now since we did our assembly and gave the speeches and showed the videos and made all the posters and leaflets and set up the drop-in center where young kids could talk to older kids about school problems, but it doesn't feel like anything really changed at all.

Mayflower Academy still has a bad name in the news for after-school fighting and some kids are still carrying knives and everyone still gets excited chatting about the time the gunshot went off at Clinton Brunton-Fletcher. And kids are still getting their phones and wallets jacked by other kids on the bus home and forming little gangs and going to get their own back — and still announcing that their street is a no-go area to kids from just two streets away then hitting each other with baseball bats and bike chains if they trespass.

And Delano's big brother Janelle and his mates were eventually arrested for another different shooting and put in juvie so, yes, that meant they couldn't come to Mayflower anymore looking for Clinton. . . . But all that did was make Delano in Year Ten feel more like a one hundred percent rudeboy 'cos his brother was like a fallen soldier locked up for defending his endz, blah blah blah blah blah BLAH.

I said all this today to Ms. Bracket when she called me into her office and she listened really carefully to it all and then she said, "Are you a bit down, Shiraz? You're very negative."

So I says, "Well, no, not negative, Ms. B, more realistic."

And she looked at me and nodded and said, "Well, we all have our own truth, I suppose." Then she thought for a bit and said, "Are you not enjoying studying?"

And I sighed and said, "Well, yeah, I'm enjoying it . . . but it's not like I'm enjoying it so much that I want to keep on doing it for another four whole years."

Ms. Bracket nodded slowly and said, "So what would you rather be doing?"

So I said, "Following my dreams and being free!"

Ms. Bracket said she understood about that and that's why she went on a gap year to Israel and worked picking grapes on a kibbutz before she went to uni, 'cos she wanted to get stuff out of her system and experience life. I stared at her for a bit then, sitting behind her desk in her smart suit with tons of files on her desk and her phone ringing off the hook, trying to imagine her seventeen years old and completely free. I couldn't.

"Anyway," said Ms. Bracket. "I disagree with you about the 'Increase the Peace' campaign. I think you did some brilliant work. The Year Sevens and Year Eights gave us some amazing feedback. They totally engaged with your message."

"Mmm," I said.

"So that's why I want you to step it up a gear," she said.

"What do you mean?" I said.

"Well, we're having the official opening of the new Sixth

Form block in April and all the national TV news crews will be there as we're having a VIP guest to unveil the plaque. So Mr. Bamblebury and I thought you and your 'Increase the Peace' team could put together a few hours of entertainment. Maybe use the new music room equipment? Speeches? A little play?"

"Who is the VIP guest?!" I said.

"Oh, no one to really worry about," she said.

"Who?" I said.

"It's His Royal Highness, Prince Charles," she said.

"Crapping hell," I said.

"Pardon?" she said.

"Nothing," I said.

MARCH

SUNDAY 1ST MARCH

From: Cavasuewhereareyou@steeldrum.com
To: Theshizz@wideblueyonder.co.uk
Subject: **Hanoi Rocks**

Hey Shiz!!! It's Cava-Sue!!! So so so so sorry I've not been any good at the whole write/text/blog/whatever thing but we are just so lost in this amazing experience that I've totally forgotten myself. Plus the Internet connection is so crap over here. I'm typing this in an Internet café beside the Cu Chu tunnels an hour from Ho Chi Minh City.

Well, I say Internet café, basically I'm sitting in someone's kitchen using a laptop and an old woman with no teeth is trying to sell me and Lewis noodles and chicken feet for 5 billion dong. Not great.

We've spent the last week in the Mekong Delta just bumbling about looking at temples and meeting real-life Vietnamese folk and going on bus and boat rides. We're heading back now to Ho Chi Minh City to see a doctor as Lewis has infected bedbug bites on his arse. I keep feeling spewy in the mornings. Think we're sick. Don't tell Mum!!!

147

Hope you're OK, Shiraz? Hope Joshua is treating you well? Are you studying hard? Send me some gossip soon! Cava-Sue xx

THURSDAY 5TH MARCH

Oh my days, I made the HUGE mistake today of telling my mother about HRH Prince Charles visiting Mayflower School. I have never seen her so happy EVER. Honestly, never ever. Not even when I told her how Maria Draper had one of them colonic irrigations and it went a bit wrong after she went through to the supermarket wearing cream trousers. Not even as happy as then.

I always forget how much my mother loves royalty. She once made me and Cava-Sue stand for four and a half hours outside Poundland in Ilford Mall just to push daffodils in Princess Anne's face. Mum loves Prince Charles even more.

"Ooh Crivens!" she was saying, "Is Charlie coming! I love Charlie! And is he bringing Camilla too? And will you get to speak to him? And what will you say!? Will it be in the newspapers! Will you get a photograph of you and Charlie standing together for the wall, Shiraz? Oh my God, I can't believe this. I've gotta call your Aunty Glo and tell her. She will die!"

Mum then got on the phone with Glo and by the time she'd talked the whole thing up it sounded like Charles was coming just to see ME in particular as he was bringing the Queen's special sword and I was in line for some type of knighthood. Mum also agreed with Glo that they'd take the day off work and come down and wave Union Jacks. Oh. My. Days.

You'd think that a bunch of folks with funny teeth and flappy ears who don't work for a living and are always getting drunk would get on Mum's nerves. When it was the Brunton-Fletchers doing it she kept a log-book of complaints and tried to get them moved to Hastings on an ASBO. But with the Royal Family it's different.

WEDNESDAY 11TH MARCH

OK, I'll come clean: I've been dragging my feet over this whole Increase-the-Peace-Prince-Charles-thing. I've been seriously busy with studying and seeing Josh. And if you want me to be properly frank I've got no bloody idea where to even start bringing the worlds of royalty and anti-gangster rap together for a national media audience type-thingy. In fact, I'm proper scared. Not that I'll admit that, 'cos I do a pretty good job around Mayflower of acting totally nails.

So anyway, I get to school today and I'm well shocked to find my Joshua has stuck up posters all around the Sixth Form saying:

INCREASE THE PEACE — ROYAL EXTRAVAGANZA — MEETING TODAY — 1PM AV ROOM

And I'm thinking, 'Ere, that's weird 'cos when I mentioned this to Joshua last week he just made all sorts of sarcastic comments about chav rap and how the Royals should all be taken round the back of the palace and shot for scrounging our money. Then

Josh said he'd already done one "Help the ASBOs" campaign and he was too busy.

But here he is today in the AV room, suddenly holding a meeting that I don't even know about, like it's all his project! So I say, "Josh, you never said you were organizing a meeting!" So Josh says, "Oh, babycakes, yes I did. You need to get your ears checked out." And I say, "No Josh, you DEFINITELY said you were too busy!" And Josh says, in front of everyone, "Shiz, seriously, book an appointment with the doctor. Those bling-bling hoops you used to wear from Ilford market have affected your eardrums!" Then everyone in the AV room burst out laughing and I tried to join in too, 'cos I didn't want him to see I was hurt. I don't even wear those hoops no more. Or my locket. Or my bracelet. Or any gold at all. Just 'cos Josh is the best-looking boy in the whole school he thinks he can say anything he wants to anyone, even to his girlfriend. I know he doesn't mean it though, he's just showboating. He's proper lovely when we're on our own.

Anyway, as soon as Sean, Luther, and Nabila and everyone arrive, Josh starts talking.

"Right everyone," he says, "So basically, we've got Prince Charles coming to the school to present a plaque, y'know, yada, yada, whatever," he says. "And there's going to be loads of national media here. So we've got to put on a bit of a show, or whatever," he says, sounding quite bored, "So I'm thinking, let's get some of the rudes in Year Ten to jump about a bit and do some of their shouting, sorry, I mean 'rapping,' then we can maybe show Prince Charles the mixing desk, then some of the other chavster kids who use the music room can do some of their tracks, then we can unveil the plaque . . ."

Everyone sort of nodded and mumbled in agreement.

"And I'm thinking," says Josh a lot more forcefully now. "That I'll help Prince Charles unveil the plaque. And I'll give a little speech about how my, I mean sorry, *our* 'Increase the Peace' campaign has turned the school's fortunes around and how we've collected loads of money. And how hard we've worked to set a good example to the younger kids and keep them in school and overcome their backgrounds, y'know, blah blah blah, that sort of thing. Agreed?!"

No one tried to argue with Josh, they all just sort of nodded. Suddenly I couldn't stop thinking about what he said in the library at Christmas about doing stuff to look good on university application forms.

"So, Shiraz?" he says. But I'm proper miles away now thinking, how can someone so handsome and funny be sometimes such a FAKER and I'm thinking about my mother saying about how Josh would need two faces and a slithering tail to be a politician. Then Josh says "SHIRAZ!" again and I say, "Sorry, what?!" Then he says, "So can you and Carrie find some Year Nines and Tens who can rap or dance or something? It doesn't matter who really. . . ."

So I say, "Well, I think if we're going to do something for Prince Charles, we should do it properly!" Then Josh just sighs and goes, "Whatever." So I say, "So I'm thinking we need to ask someone to help us this time who we never asked last time.

Someone who really knows about street-culture and all that type of stuff. We need to ask Uma to get involved."

"Uma Brunton-Fletcher?!" said Joshua.

"Uma Brunton-Fletcher," I said. "'Cos at least she knows what she's talking about. I think we need this whole thing to sound, y'know, like we mean it? Like we're being sincere. Like we're not FAKERS."

Josh just ignored the word *faker*. Like I wasn't meaning him.

I asked Uma. She is properly over the moon. She's already started making plans. Joshua says we can all do what we bloody want, but he's definitely helping Prince Charles unveil the plaque. End of.

FRIDAY 13TH MARCH

Well Friday the 13th was certainly proper unlucky for Carrie Draper today. She's had an official warning from Mayflower Sixth Form about her attendance. Mr. Bamblebury has written to Barney and said that unless Carrie gets doctor's notes to cover the "myriad of unfortunate allergies, infections, and trans-viral airbound superbugs she has suffered from this term," then they will NOT put her in for her AS-Level exams.

Barney Draper has gone mental! He even tried to stop her seeing Saf, but then Carrie shouted at him that this was just typical of him using that to stop her dating Saf as he is SUCH A BLOODY RACIST!!! Then Barney, who isn't a racist at all, totally caved in and let her out. Carrie says she don't give a crap about Sixth Form. Carrie says that if Barney gives her his business she's going to flog it and start up her own beauty school just like Tabitha Tennant.

I don't think she was joking.

SUNDAY 15TH MARCH

Nan and Clement have booked Romford Registry Office on the first Saturday in July for their wedding! I am going to be a bridesmaid! And our Murphy is going to be best man! Murphy and Clement have formed quite a bond recently over their love of sitting about eating cakes and watching films about war. Clement has even learned to get to Level 3 of *Decapitation Nation* on PS2. And that's not bad for an old geezer with rheumatoid arthritis in one wrist.

WEDNESDAY 18TH MARCH

Well, tonight was properly mental. I've got so much to think about now. My head is going to explode. So basically, we're doing the "Increase the Peace" Prince Charles presentation on Thursday 9th April — which leaves us, like, three weeks to get it all together and none of us have done anything 'cos we were going to do it last weekend but we all went to a shubz instead in Chadwell Heath 'cos this girl Martika who used to go to Mayflower was celebrating her eighteenth birthday and she had this proper amazing party in her garage and kids came from all over Essex and it all got well messy.

Basically, I lost Joshua completely and Carrie had a fight with

Saf and Sean met a boy from the Isle of Dogs and Nabila drank a Breezer and wore false eyelashes with her hijab which is strictly forbidden by Allah and we were all dancing and being stupid and it was a proper amazing night. But the end result is that we've done nothing about Prince Charles whatsoever. Sorry Charlie.

So we're all round at Josh's house tonight for an "Increase the Peace" meeting, sitting in his big living-room/dining-room area which is all pure white walls and polished bare floorboards with a massive oak dining table and bookshelves full of books and vases with one single tropical flower sticking out of them and copies of posh furniture magazines lying about on a posh coffee table that doesn't look like it ever had a cup of coffee on it in its life.

Me and Josh and Luther and Sean and Nabila are all sitting round the oak table talking about how behind we are with schoolwork and Josh is moaning on about how he's never going to get into Oxford if his marks aren't good, he's going to have to go somewhere crap like Durham or Edinburgh. Then his mother appears wearing a navy blue apron over navy trousers and her hair in a weird turban thing, giving us all the evils, which I can never tell if she really means or whether her face is just naturally stuck like she's just smelled a bad fart.

And I don't bother saying hello to her this time as I've tried loads of times and I always get the same reaction, no matter how much I try to not wear my gold or not wear my scrunchie or not wear my hoodie, she still treats me like I'm NOT A REAL BLOODY PERSON at all and always starts talking about Josh's good friends in North West London who I've still never met and then she always starts talking about her friend Jocasta's daughter

Claudia who is "asking after Josh again." So to be quite honest, I'm not bothering with Mrs. Fallow, I'm more interested at this moment in Josh's neck 'cos now I can see him in the direct sunlight sitting with his back to the patio doors I can see there is a mark on his neck that LOOKS JUST LIKE A HICKEY. And I haven't given my Josh a lovebite. 'Cos as I say, he went missing at Martika's shubz and I've not seen him much since then at all.

And I want to kick off and leave but just then the doorbell rings and I go and look out of the bay windows and it's Uma. And Uma is looking one hundred percent how Uma likes to look and she's not compromising for anyone, certainly not Mrs. snooty Fallow.

Uma's got on footless leopard-print tights and a denim miniskirt with black snakeskin pumps and a skin-tight white cropped T-shirt which shows her belly-button ring. She's got on an electric pink hoodie, two sets of big gold hoops and her gold clown pendant. She's wearing her gold charm bracelet and carrying a massive white fake Mulberry handbag from Ilford market. Uma is standing in the front garden by Josh's mother's row of recycling boxes, finishing off a Marlboro Red, and as Josh gets to the door, she shouts, "Zeus! Come on!" and Zeus comes trotting in behind her doing his best devil dog impression ever. For some reason, I want to cheer, because the thing I love about Uma is she ALWAYS keeps it real.

Well, it all starts going off then, 'cos Uma strides in and Zeus pads in after her and she shouts, "Sit down, Zeus!" which Zeus does 'cos he's actually properly trained ever since Uma's little brother shoplifted *Dog Whisperer* on DVD for Uma's Christmas pressie. So Uma's been doing the whole command/reward thing and Zeus has been learning it. Well, Uma sits down and gets out her laptop from the massive handbag and clicks a bit and logs into Josh's WiFi broadband and starts showing us all the MySpaces and Facebooks of kids at Mayflower who make music already and she's talking proper fast about e-mails she's sent and who she's heard back from. And we're sitting there, proper amazed at how much she's achieved.

Then Uma starts saying that what we need is some people who are a bit more professional to help out, y'know, like local rap artists who have a big name on the local pirate radio stations like the Crowley Park Brapboys and the Rinse and Go Fraternity? Maybe folks like that could do a little collaboration with the Year Sevens and Eights? Then Uma says that she's having no luck getting in touch with them but didn't Carrie and Shiraz's exboyfriends Bezzie Kelleher and Wesley Barrington Bains II used to know all these people really well? In fact, didn't they used to lay down tracks with them when they were in the G-Mayes Detonators? It's people like that we need to really help out, she says.

So Carrie says to me, "Well, we could ring Wesley and Bezzie and ask, couldn't we?" And I say, "Errrrm, dunnno about that." And Joshua bursts out laughing and says "Wesley Barrington Bains II!! Ha ha ha, are there two of him?" So I say, "Shut up, Joshua. Just shut up!" but Joshua is proper wetting himself going, "The G-Mayes Detonators! I've heard it all now! Ha ha ha ha!"

"Oh, just shut it!" I say. "And anyway what's that bloody mark on your neck?!"

And at that point there is a huge, ear-splitting scream in the kitchen and it's Mrs. Fallow howling, "Oh my God! Oh my God! Joshua, call the police! Call the animal control! There is a rottweiler in my kitchen! A ROTTWEILER! Call the dog-catcher! And it's eating my Portuguese Pasteis de Natas that I've baked for my book club! Aaaaaaaaaghhhhhhh!"

So we all run into the kitchen and Mrs. Fallow is standing on the kitchen table flapping her arms and crying and Uma tries to catch Zeus but he is properly distracted by the Portuguese jam tart things and Mrs. Fallow is shouting, "Get it out! Get that rottweiler out of here! Call the police!" And in the end Uma shouts, "Oh, shut your trap you silly cow, it's only a Staffy!" and Mrs. Fallow goes PROPERLY BERSERK then and chucks us all out and somehow in the confusion poor Zeus forgot all the things he learned from his *Dog Whisperer* DVD and he ended up taking a wee right up the front of Mrs. Fallow's Aga cupboard thing.

But it's made of iron, I'm sure it'll wipe clean. Some people are so dramatic.

APRIL

THURSDAY 9TH APRIL

34, Thundersley Road,
Goodmayes,
Essex,
IG5 2XS

Dear Wesley Barrington Bains II,

I'm writing this letter to you, but I pretty much one hundred percent know that I'll never send it. I just need to write stuff down to make things clearer in my head.

So much totally mental stuff has happened over the last few months that my brain is in a proper spin. Well, anyway, I was watching the morning shows the other day before school and this agony aunt was saying the best thing to do with feelings is write them in a letter then set fire to it, so the feelings can get some "closure." So that's what I'm going to do. Right, here goes.

First of all, Wesley, thank you so so so much for helping us out with the "Increase the Peace" campaign. When Uma started saying that we should call you and Bezzie up, well I was like, NO WAY, UMA, 'cos I thought you'd be all moody with me and would hold a grudge. But you didn't, Wes. You were proper lovely and chatty and helpful and you totally saved our lives. I was bricking it that Tuesday last month when me and Carrie came over to Bezzie's on Dawson Drive to chat to you both about the Prince Charles thing.

But then we gets to Bezzie's house and Bezzie opens the door and Bezzie's ancient King Charles Spaniel, Shane – who is somehow still alive 'cos he must be about 102 – runs out and starts trying to give me a paw and lick my face and Bezzie's mother starts shouting to shut the door 'cos there's a draft and it felt well weird 'cos it was exactly like when I very first met you. Everything was exactly the same, except now everything was totally different 'cos I've totally broke your heart.

So I walk up the stairs into Bezzie's room and there you are sitting on Bezzie's bed in your white Hackett sweatshirt and Nike trackie pants and your Von Dutch cap reading *Super Street* car magazine, smelling of Burberry aftershave and we start talking and my heart is beating really quick 'cos I'm nervous and I can tell you're nervous too 'cos your top lip is all sweaty. And you're like, "Hello, Shiraz Bailey Wood." And I'm like "Hello, Wesley Barrington Bains II!" and quickly we've settled into taking the mickey out of each other and you never mention Joshua Fallow once at all and that's proper good of you Wesley 'cos if you'd left me for another bird I'd never have let you forget it, mate. I'd have added her name into every single sentence. In fact, I wouldn't have spoken to you ever again at all.

I don't deserve a friend as properly lovely as you.

I can't believe you could just put all that stuff out of your head and get on and help us out. If it wasn't for you and Bezzie we'd never have talked the Rinse and Go Fraternity into coming to our school and performing a track with the Year Sevens. And we'd DEFINITELY never have talked the Crowley Park Brapboys into coming to Mayflower and doing a little collaboration with Delano and Meatman in Year Ten. In fact, without you making some phone calls and giving us some lifts in your car and basically being properly support-ive, well, I reckon we'd have had nothing to show Prince Charles at all.

That said, maybe that would have suited Prince Charles down to the ground 'cos he had a face like a drizzly day on Walthamstow Market right through the lot of it. In fact, I reckon if he'd had a choice between listening to the Rinse and Go/Year Seven track again or dying slowly of full-blown cat AIDS I think the AIDS might have won hands down, but that don't matter Wes 'cos we're still going to be in all the newspapers tomorrow and we're still all over BBC today with that Max Blackford dude going on about "An amazing change of fortune for Mayflower School who were once a bleak and war-torn establishment." 'Cos, y'know, I'm not saying we changed the world today or nothing but for one day in Mayflower Academy everyone got on and the peace was temporarily increased and there was hope. And we need some hope right now 'cos for some mental reason kids are stabbing and shooting each other all over London right now over nothing and it's heavy as hell. I think what we did to-day was amazing.

The thing that totally gets my head properly flummoxed about me and you, Wesley, is that although we are totally different in loads of ways and you reckon I've changed loads and got right up myself, well, the thing is we're also totally, exactly the same too.

Like today for example, from the second you arrived at Mayflower, I knew you were sort of seeing things in the same way as me. 'Cos we're from the same place and we're from the same type of family and same type of background and we find the same type of stuff funny and we notice the same type of stuff going on about us that other folks don't. From the very first moment I ever met you sitting on that bed in Bezzie's house the other year it was just like one big, long, silly conversation about stuff. 'Cos me and you Wesley, we just sort of gel.

So I knew today that you were finding the same type of stuff bare jokes, like the way the school all smelled of fresh paint 'cos Mr. Bamblebury had been flying about with a paint can himself that morning. And the way there was suddenly no litter or grafitti anywhere 'cos old Bumbleclot had been up all night scrubbing it off. And the way the cafeteria ladies were all wearing lipstick and fresh clean pink smocks and not looking like bloody lesser-spotted Mexican swamp-donkeys as usual. And how all these total nutters have started appearing at the school gate clutching Union Jacks and tea towels, including my mother who has been lurking outside the school with Aunty Glo since 7:30AM wearing a T-shirt that says, CHARLIE IS MY DARLING that she's had in her wardrobe since she camped outside Buckingham Palace for the Royal Wedding in 1981! Properly shameful I know!!!

But the thing is Wes, I'm not ashamed about my family when it comes to you 'cos your family are just like that too. 'Cos you've got a mad Uncle Terry who reckons he's Batman who drives about Ilford in a battered old Subaru playing proper loud Madness on his stereo. And you've got a daft Aunty Lil who's married to a Pearly King and she walks around Bermondsey on Sundays in a jacket and big hat covered in buttons collecting money for a kiddie's charity.

And you've got a bonkers godmother, Sheila, who's proper obsessed with *Phantom of the Opera* who always wears an official baseball cap and sweatshirt and runs the Internet fan club from her extra room. And your mum is always showing me the latest two-for-one bargain she bought down at Food Lion. And you don't think it's weird that we own a Staffy and all our friends own Staffies (sometimes two or three Staffies each!!) or that I knock about with someone who has a fridge in their front garden, or that we all decorate the front of our houses at Christmas or that no one in my house has ever been to university ever or that all the women on my street wear a lot of gold, because the thing is, Wesley, they're all like that on your street too.

I miss that, Wesley. I don't have that with Joshua Fallow.

But the thing is, Wesley Barrington Bains II, although we are totally the same in lots of ways, we are also properly different too.

And I don't know why that is, Wes, sometimes I just think

that maybe our brains are wired up different. 'Cos ever since I started doing well at school in Year Eleven, my brain started properly racing ahead to learn the next thing and I started working out where I could go with it all and thinking and thinking and thinking about the whole big world out there and my part in it and you don't really think like that at all, do you?

You think it's proper weird when I want to buy a big newspaper or if I want to find out about other people's religions or that I think it's totally OK if Nabila Chaalan's mother wants to walk about in head-to-foot Niqib if that's what makes her happy or if Danny Braffman wants to grow the biggest Jew-fro hairdo this side of Stamford Hill and his mother wants to wear a wig that is exactly like her normal hair 'cos it's her religion. Or if Sean Burton wants to turn up to meet Prince Charles in a pink T-shirt with a big rainbow on the front and then do a rap which rhymes the words "King Lear" with "totally queer" that gets such a loud sucking of teeth from the whole of the Year Ten rudes that I think he's going to get knocked backward off the stage with the sonic boom of noise. Even you were tutting too, Wesley.

But Sean Burton don't care 'cos he is proud to be different and I'm proud of him too. I reckon you've got to live and let live, Wes. There's so much out there in the big wide world, Wesley, and I want to find out about it all 'cos I'm proper curious and I don't just mean about schoolbooks and Shakespeare, I mean real life, real people, real situations, and real experiences and you don't want to have them, do you? You don't want to see the real world outside Essex at all. You don't want to stand on Waterloo Bridge and feel alive.

Do you?

But, whatever. The one thing that today's events have made me see, Wesley Barrington Bains II, is that you've always got my back. You're always looking out for me and there's not many folks in this world I can say that about, 'cos as far as I can see in this life, you've got your family and you've got maybe one or two other folks who would honestly give half a crap if you got squashed by a falling piano or run over by a herd of startled gazelles. And one of them folks in my life is you. I'm proper scared, Wes, that I'll mess this up with you and then there won't be no others.

'Cos like today, you could see how pissed-off Joshua Fallow was getting when he wasn't getting no attention at all from the TV crews or the teachers or Prince Charles during the "Increase the Peace" assembly. You could see that he was starting to take it out on me. Especially when Uma got up in her hoops and her mini and gave her little speech about Mayflower becoming a Center of Excellence and how teachers like Ms. Bracket had totally given her a chance and turned her life about and she wanted to carry on in education.

Well, everyone loved that and people were clapping and Prince Charles was nodding – well at least I reckon he was nodding unless he was having problems keeping his head upright due to the weight of his big ears – and all the papers wanted to take pictures of Uma and interview Uma for the TV news and everyone remembered Uma's bit of the day and

NOTHING about the fact that Joshua was up on the stage beside Prince Charles when he unveiled the plaque. No one remembered Joshua's part in things at all. And as soon as the assembly was over Joshua started having a proper go at me, saying, "Oh brilliant, Shiraz, now everyone thinks Uma organized this whole thing! That looks great, doesn't it?"

So I laugh and say, "Well Uma did organize it! She had all the ideas! She's been working every night on it! All you did was hang about trying to get on Sky News so it looks good on your Oxford University application!" So then Joshua just snorts and says, "Well, I should have known all you chav-scummers would stick together." So I goes, "Who are you calling chav scum?! You bloody snobby-nosed prat." So Joshua just laughs and says, "Look, Shiraz, I don't think this whole relationship thing is working out, is it? I don't think we're very compatible?"

So I got proper cross then and shouts, "No, Joshua, I don't think we're very compatible 'cos you keep turning up at school on Mondays with hickies, saying they're eczema!" So Joshua just laughs and says, "Look, I'm going to be totally honest with you, Shiraz, 'cos I know you respect people 'keeping it real' and not being 'fakers' and all the chav warrior blah-blah-crap. I've been seeing Claudia in Hampstead, my mum's friend's daughter. I need to break things off."

Well, I was totally stunned. I wasn't expecting that and I don't know how 'cos now I think about it it's totally obvious. Josh didn't even look embarrased. "I know there's been a bit of an overlap," he said. "But you understand, don't you? Yeah? Good."

And then he walked off. Just like that.

So I walked out of the Sixth Form block and sat on the bench by the parking lot and my face felt red and my head felt dizzy and I wanted to cry but I couldn't. And that's when you came out and sat on the bench and put your arm around me and didn't say anything for ages and then you made me get into the passenger seat of your banana-yellow Golf and you drove me home to my mum at Thundersley Road.

So thank you for all of that, Wesley Barrington Bains II. Thank you.

I am properly mixed up about how I feel about everything right now, and to be honest writing it all down has only made me feel more confused.

But I suppose the one thing I do know for sure is if I was to get squashed by a piano or trampled by a herd of startled gazelles tomorrow I would go to my grave having known what it feels like to feel properly, properly loved.

I need to burn this letter now.

Lots of love, now and forever,

Shiraz Bailey Woodxxxxxxx

MAY

MONDAY 4TH MAY

OH MY GOSH. Carrie has been chucked out of Mayflower Sixth Form Center of Excellence.

Mr. Bumbleclot has finally snapped and terminated her pupil contract. He simply refuses to believe Carrie was off on Thursday and Friday due to the Ministry of Agriculture running tests to see if her sore throat was the human strain of Taiwanese bird flu.

"A laughable history of preposterous lies and excuses" — that's how our headmaster described Carrie's general attendance in his letter to Barney Draper. (It's harsh, but sort of true.)

Well, Barney Draper has hit the bloody roof. He's gone totally 110 percent radio-rental-mental-shouting-and-screaming-kkkkrrraazy. He's gone that sort of mental your mum and dad go when you know if they could actually get away with walloping you they'd just bloody do it, 'cos you've pushed them so far that they're just standing there shouting like loonies and they're not even making sense at times and their eyes are so big you actually think "crapping hell they're going to have a heart attack and I don't know any first aid."

That sort of mental.

My mum used to get like that all the time with Cava-Sue. Well, until Cava-Sue started living 5,000 miles away and then all of a sudden my mother rewrites history with Cava-Sue as some sort of saint, and not someone who is basically getting drunk in bars across Australia and passing it off as "world exploration."

So anyway, Carrie calls me this morning at 8:30AM crying her eyes out going, "That pig Bamblebury has chucked me out of Sixth Form! My dad is doing his nut! Come over and save me!" So I pull on my hoodie and my jeans and get over to Draperville and the electric gates are stood open for some reason so I wander in and right away I hear ONE HELLUVA bloody fight going on and I follow the noise round to the swimming pool and there's Maria Draper standing on the terrace wearing a beige velour tracksuit and pink flip flops with Alexis their chihuahua under her arm, shouting, "Will the two of you bloody get inside now! The neighbors can hear every word!"

So I look over by the pool and there's Carrie in her nightie standing on top of a patio table underneath the pool cabana screaming at Barney Draper, "I hate you! I hate you! I wish I'd never been born! You don't know who I am! You think you do but you don't! Get away from me, you bloody pig!" And Barney is there in his work clothes: trackie bottoms, old Lacoste T-shirt, and tool belt, shouting, "And you can get down off that table too before you break it! You spoiled little brat! Where do you think this all comes from? Do you think it grows on trees! No, I work day and night! Day and bloody night! And I built this whole place up from scratch! I had nothing when I was your age! NOTHING! Not a bloody pot to piss in! I've worked my arse off for TWENTY BLOODY YEARS for you and your mother! Now look at you, you lazy little brat! You could have all of this on a plate! But you don't

174

want it! Oh no! All you had to do was get some qualifications then it was yours! But you don't want to work! You make me sick!"

Then Carrie, whose face is bright red, shouts, "OH, SHUT UP! Shut up! You stupid bloody man! I hate you! I don't want any of this! I didn't ask for any of this! And I'm not bloody interested in running a Jacuzzi installation bloody business! I don't want it! It's boring! You can't make me be something you want me to be, you bloody headbending, brainwashing weirdo! I should get social services on you! You won't let me be who I want to be! I just want to be me! I don't need you and your head-control!"

So Barney's laughing now, but not funny laughing, angry laughing, 'Oh, you don't want none of this, do you?!" he's shouting. "Do you!?? You don't want your allowance? You don't want the widescreen TV in your room and your iPod and your gym membership and that running tab I keep settling at Cheeky's Vertical Tanning Salon and the bags full of designer outfits I seem to keep paying for! You don't want me being your bloody ATM, do you!? I should get a fizzing key-pad fitted to my chest! You're a little leech! If you don't want none of this then pack your bags! Go and stand on your own two feet!"

So Carrie screams, "Oh, don't worry about it! I will! I'm leaving now! I'm going to live at Shiraz's house!"

Then she jumps off the pool cabana table and storms upstairs and packs a wheelie suitcase full of clothes and leaves Draperville, slamming the front door. As I write this, she's having a nap in Cava-Sue's old room.

My mother says Carrie's welcome to stay until things calm

down. Or until she realizes that our house has no swimming pool facilities or in-room TV. Whichever is soonest.

THURSDAY 7TH MAY

Carrie is still living with us at the Wood household. It's pretty good having her here, but she is a proper distraction schoolwork-wise. Carrie says she feels so amazingly free now she don't have to think about English AS-Level. Carrie says it's just enough having her whole life ahead of her with no one planning it for her! Carrie says it feels like a big weight's been lifted off her mind and she's going to build herself up from nothing like Tabitha Tennant did. I ask her how she's going to do that and she says she's still figuring it out.

Then Carrie asked to borrow three quid off me for bus fares to Saf's house 'cos Barney has cut off the direct deposit into her savings account. Carrie only went out to Saf's 'cos my mum was saying it was her turn to shovel up the dog turds in the backyard. Carrie don't do dog poo.

FRIDAY 8TH MAY

Joshua Fallow and Claudia Ravenscroft's families are both going on holiday together this July. They're going to Claudia's granny's summer house in Tuscany. Joshua says he isn't in love with Claudia because let's face it they're both going off to uni next year so they can't get into anything heavy. It's just fun for now, Joshua says.

The thing is about Claudia, Joshua says, is that she's just cool.

She just sort of gets where he's coming from. Their familes are sort of the same, Joshua says. Joshua doesn't say this sort of thing about Claudia directly to me. He says it to whoever is sitting beside him in English when I'm trying to concentrate on Shakespeare and not think about quitting school. School really sucks right now.

SUNDAY 10TH MAY

I went to Ilford Mall with my nan today to find her a bridal outfit. Murphy came too and went to Marks and Spencer with Clement. My mother chucked Murphy some money before they went and said, "And come back with something smart! Not something a bum would put on for a court appearance!"

I can't believe she trusted Murphy to buy his own outfit. Then again, I suppose he has grown up a lot over the last year. He spends all his time now texting Rema and he's even giving Delano and Meatman a wide berth. He's actually quite mature. I can't help thinking it was the "Naughty Babes" calendar that did it.

Nan and Clement are so in love with each other. They walk about together holding hands and they finish each other's sentences and they just seem to know what the other one is thinking all the time. It makes me feel odd when I'm with them 'cos I feel properly on my own. My nan asked me if I wanted to bring a young man to her wedding so I have someone to dance with and carry me home when I've got blisters. I said I'd have a think.

Me and Nan went into Marks and Spencer to choose her hat when Clement wasn't looking. The assistant asked her what sort of color she was looking for and Nan said, "I want something really gay!" The assistant nearly fell over backward with shock, so I explained my nan meant "lively and happy and fun" 'cos that's what gay used to mean, last time Nan got married. I like hanging about with Nan and Clement, they're from another world.

FRIDAY 15TH MAY

Barney Draper came to collect Carrie from our house tonight. He picked her up in his work van and took her to Spirit of Siam for some noodles. Just like they always used to do on Fridays when she was in Year Eight, Nine, and Ten, back when she was a little girl and she wasn't out with boyfriends and she was basically Barney's little princess and didn't give him tons of earache all the time.

Carrie was in Cava-Sue's old bedroom when Barney tooted the horn, packing her clothes and all her Tabitha Tennant beauty manuals into her wheelie suitcase. I told Carrie she didn't have to go if she didn't want to. I told her my mum was only kidding when she said she had to unblock the hair from the upstairs sink. Carrie said thanks for everything and she's proper grateful but she's decided to go home to Draperville to begin Stage One of her new life plan.

I said to Carrie that I thought Stage One of her new plan was going to involve standing on her own two feet. Carrie said she definitely has a plan up her sleeve and it did involve all that independence-blah-blah type-thing, but there was no harm in planning it from her own bedroom in Draperville.

I gave her a hug, then I watched as she walked out of the front door and down the path. Barney got out of the van and leaned against it with his arms crossed as she sauntered toward him proper sulkily.

He picked up the pink suitcase without a word and put it into the back of his van. Then they both scowled at each other for a bit, having a sort of stand-off. Then she poked him in the stomach and he burst out laughing, then he grabbed her by the waist and swung her round and round until she started squealing with laughter, then she jumped in the passenger seat and they drove off.

I have no bloody idea what she's going to do next.

FRIDAY 22ND MAY

OK — it's sort of mad 'cos I honestly don't really know how this whole thing with Wesley Barrington Bains II has started happening again, but it just sort of has.

Well, to be honest, I'm not sure it really has but everyone else in the world seems to think so, including Wesley and both of our mothers, who will have plenty to discuss on their next rendezvous in the Food Lion aisle.

I don't remember agreeing to anything. All I said in my text was that I'd go out for a pizza with Wesley just for a chat and a laugh, just like friends would 'cos that's what we are, good friends.

So I'm in my bedroom tonight ironing my hair and putting on lip gloss when all of a sudden there's a right fuss going on downstairs, so I know Wesley has arrived to pick me up. Straight-away my mother is up opening the front door and my brother is outside looking at the new spoiler Wesley's put on the car and my dad's outside on the path looking as happy as happy can be.

And by the time I come down Wesley's sitting in the lounge, with his feet up on the special leather ottoman that my mother bought in the DFS Furniture Showroom May Sale that's only to be used for special occasions and he's got a cup of tea in one hand and a handful of Cadbury's animal crackers in the other. Everyone turned to smile at me when I walked through the door like something genuinely amazing was happening. We were only going for a pizza at Pizza Junction, not to the Registry Office!

"Ooh, Wesley's just telling us about his condo he's buying!" my mum was saying, "Just down the road it is! You could walk there in twenty minutes from here!"

"Mmm, I know," I said, putting in my gold hoops.

"Well, that's such a sensible thing to do with your money, Wesley," my mum was saying. "Your dad would be very proud. So is it a ground-floor apartment or upstairs? I mean . . . could you have kids in it if you wanted at some point?"

"Come on, Wesley," I said, dragging him out of the door.

We arrived at Pizza Junction and then we sat in the green racing car which is Wesley's favorite 'cos when you honk the buzzer for service it plays the tune "Yankee-Doodle-Dandy." We talked about his plumbing NVQ and some tracks he's been laying down with Bezzie that are up on their MySpace and some big car meet that they're both going to next weekend in Southend that I can go to if I want. We had a good time really, I suppose. And when he drove me home to Thundersley Road we sat outside for a bit and chatted and when he leaned over to give me a kiss I didn't push him away or nothing I just let him kiss me on the mouth. It didn't feel funny or nothing, it just felt like it always used to.

Just like we'd never ever split up.

JUNE

TUESDAY 9TH JUNE

I did an English AS-Level exam today. Oh my days, I was bricking it before I went to school. Everybody in the family was too. I must have been giving off some serious runnybum vibes around the house. Well, in the rare moments I've actually been spotted over the last few weeks.

I've been trapped in that bloody bedroom with my head in a book for almost a fortnight solid. I've only been appearing to yell at Murphy about playing his Dubstep or on one occasion to cut the plug off Glo's karaoke machine. (Saying that, it wasn't just me upset about last Saturday night. When Glo sang "Wind Beneath My Wings" with all the windows open a lot of folks reckoned it was Bert's wife at number 89 getting committed again.)

I could hardly speak for nerves when I got to school today. I just sat there with Uma in the common room clutching my pen and my pencil and my spare pen and my lucky fluffy hedgehog that Wesley bought me. My stomach kept on trying to make an escape through my gob so I had to sit there still with my lips tight shut. Then Joshua rolls in and he's being his usual mega-mega-confident self, just strutting around chatting about next year when he's doing his A2s and what him and Claudia have been up to and how he got scouted in the street the other day to be a model by Storm but he said no thanks, 'cos, like, he wants to be a politician or a PR guru like his dad or something, yada-yada-yada.

So we all went into the exam room and sat down and I was sitting next to Manpreet, so he's setting all his pens and pencils out in dead straight lines 'cos he's got Asperger's (it's finally been officially diagnosed at last), and Uma is behind me and I can hear her foot tapping and her gob chewing gum like crazy. Then I turn over the paper and the first question I see is:

"Is King Lear 'more sinned against than sinning'?" Give examples, trying to examine the motives for each character's behavior and judging who is the victim of each situation.

And my heart went BOOM BOOM BOOM!!! when I saw that, because I'd revised something a bit like it about five times round at Uma's, and I know she knew it too. So I starts scribbling away like mad writing about Lear's love test and when he was cast out into the storm and the suicide of Cordelia etc., etc., etc.

And when I look over at Josh, he's not really writing much. He's just staring at the paper and looking a bit annoyed. A bit flustered. Like it wasn't a question he's ever thought about. HA HA HA HA HA.

I mean, I'm sure he did OK in the end. But thinking that he must have got his arse kicked on that paper by "chav-scummers" like me and Uma has cheered me up no end.

FRIDAY 12TH JUNE

Today was European History AS-Level. Sigh. I think it went fine. I mean I don't think I got an A or anything 'cos, y'know, how the hell are you meant to know every piddly little thing about a period of history?? It's impossible. But at least there were plenty of questions about Ferdinand of Spain and about Martin Luther giving the pope an earache over his grievances, so I reckon what I did was OK.

Wesley picked me up in his car after the exam and took me for a burger. Wesley says his lawyer who is helping him buy the condo called today and said the contracts have been "exchanged." This means the condo is 99% definitely his.

Wesley says that if I ever move in I'd love living there. Wesley says the second bedroom, that I can use for my books or something until we have kids, looks over the loading bay of the pakora factory. "So that's pretty cool, innit?" Wesley says. "'Cos there'll always be something interesting for us both to look at."

WEDNESDAY 17TH JUNE

I did my Critical Thinking paper today. It wasn't too bad. I was half expecting to turn it over and for it simply to say "PEDOS ARE OK?: DISCUSS" but it didn't. Instead there were tons of multiple choice questions about whether cigarette advertising was responsible for lung cancer, or whether folks who treat their dogs the same as humans could be called "crazy."

I tried to answer them my very best but to be honest my head was hurting and I was feeling proper tired and confused. I finished the exam and went over to see Carrie at Draperville and now I'm more confused than ever.

Carrie had called me after the exam in a right weird mood saying she had finally worked out Stage One of the Carrie Draper "Whole New Me" plan and she needed to tell me STRAIGHT AWAY, like NOW. So I went over not expecting too much 'cos ever since Carrie was turfed out of Mayflower Sixth Form her daily routine seems to have consisted of (a) watching Lifetime TV, (b) dehairing various parts of her legs, arms, top lip etc. and (c) lying about in a robe waiting for various nail polishes to dry.

So I get to Draperville and Carrie's in the pool cabana and the first thing she says to me is, "What are you doing with your life, Shiraz Bailey Wood?" And I sigh and say, "Looking at someone with bleach cream on their top lip?" And Carrie goes, "No, not now face-ache, for the rest of your life? Forever?"

So I go, "Oh? That? Oh, I don't bloody know. Stay on at school for another year I suppose? If I can. Dunno. Maybe go to uni . . . something like that."

So Carrie goes, "Yeah, you sound proper THRILLED about that." And I say, "Hmm, you know I'm not thrilled. I'm bored sick of being locked in that room studying. And I ain't got no choice really but to carry on 'cos if I don't I'm going to end up living behind an Indian food factory with Wesley Barrington Bains II." So Carrie goes, "Hang on? So are you officially back together with Wesley then?" And I go, "Hmm, sort of. Wesley just acts like we never even split up. He won't talk about Joshua. He just calls it "those months when Shiraz had the hump."

There was a long silence while we both sat for a bit watching Alexis the dog rolling about on the lawn.

"He loves me, y'know?" I said to Carrie after a while, knowing how crap that made me sound.

"Oh, Shiraz," said Carrie. Then she got a glossy magazine out of her bag. It had a picture of Tabitha Tennant on the front dressed in a white coat. The title of the brochure was:

BUTTERZ BEAUTY ACADEMY
COVENT GARDEN
LONDON WC1
OFFICIAL PROSPECTUS

"That's Tabitha Tennant's beauty school, isn't it?" I said.

"Yeah!" smiled Carrie, almost fizzing with happiness.

"Eh? Have you applied to go?" I said.

"I applied three weeks ago. When I moved from your house back to here," Carrie said. "I talked my dad into lending me the money for my course fees!"

"Oh my God!" I said.

"And I didn't want to say anything," said Carrie. " 'Cos if it all went wrong I'd look even more stupid. . . . But I had my final interview yesterday. And I got in, Shiraz! I bloody got in! I'm moving to London! I'm going to be a trainee at Tabitha Tennant's Butterz Beauty Academy! I'm so excited! I can't believe it!"

I just stared at her with my gob open.

I felt well happy for her but also a bit shocked and a little tiny bit sad too.

"You're moving to London!?" I said.

"Yeah! In a few weeks' time!" she said.

"But . . . but . . . !" I started to stutter, but my head was proper racing. I was starting to feel a bit jealous now too. Imagine actually moving to London? Imagine having your own place and being right in the middle of everything? You could stand on Waterloo Bridge every day if you liked! And if you wanted to paddle in the Trafalgar Square fountains and go to the club every night, you could! Imagine that though? Imagine that?????

I've been imagining that for months and months.

"Come with me, Shiraz," she said.

"What?" I said. "How? I can't!"

"What do you mean, you can't?" she said.

"I can't just leave Goodmayes! I can't," I said.

"Yes you can!" said Carrie, "Come with me and we'll get a little apartment and you can get a job and I'll go to Butterz Beauty Academy and we can have a walloping big adventure!"

"But —" I said.

"Oh come on, Shizza, there's nothing round here for us! Nothing. I'm sick of going to the same places all the time. I'm sick of seeing Saf all the time too. That's all getting way too bloody serious. I want to have some fun!"

"But I can't just leave," I said. "I can't do something like that."

Because I can't do that. Can I?

Can I???

JULY

FRIDAY 3RD JULY

You wouldn't think an almost seventy-four-year-old woman would end up with a right old rowdy hen night, but when it comes to my family nothing is ever quiet.

"Ooh, I don't want no fuss!" my nan kept saying, but I think deep down she did really. Well, least I hope she did 'cos as soon as my Aunty Glo got her beak in we ended up with a roped-off bit of Goodmayes Social for Nan and me, Carrie, Mum, Glo, Betty, Peggy, and all the other old girls from Nan's Wednesday club.

Everyone was chatting and laughing and drinking cocktails with rude names and wearing tiaras and line-dancing and making a right old fuss.

I've got to admit, when Glo said she had a couple of very special surprises for Nan and that Nan had to "bring her best glasses 'cos it was going to be quite a sight," I thought, "Oh my days, no, Glo, what have you done?!" And sure enough, she never let me down.

'Cos at about 9PM, with the drinks and silliness in full flow, this young bloke appears wearing a funny wig and glasses and a sparkly jacket dressed a bit like that singer Elton John. Then he sits down at the piano and we're all staring at him thinking, "'Ere, mate, you weren't invited!" then he starts to play and sing that well-serious song by Elton John called "Rocket Man."

So we all think, "Fair enough," and we're all laughing and singing along . . . and then smoke begins to come out of his trousers. SMOKE! Big clouds of it! Like his pants were on fire! And we're all beginning to get proper hysterical by this point. And with that, some loud disco music began to kick in through the speakers and the bloke leaped up from the piano seat, ripped his trousers off in one go and underneath he had a pair of gold underpants with a message on them that said THE ROCKET MAN!!!

He was a stripper! Then he began doing a rude dance around the social club, rubbing his bum against Nan's friends' cardigans and threatening to dangle his wotnots in their port! Well, honestly, we all nearly died laughing! Especially Nan, who had to have a shot of her asthma inhaler she was laughing so much. Glo looked very proud of herself.

Then just as things couldn't get any more surreal, the smoke began to clear and I saw by the bar, the biggest surprise of all. It was Cava-Sue! My big sister Cava-Sue! Standing at the bar with her backpack. So I turned to Glo and said, "Is that our Cava-Sue?! But she's in Australia, isn't she?" But Glo just winked, so she must have known she was coming all along.

Well, me and Mum and Nan all ran across the room and gave Cava-Sue a big hug and said how proper crafty she was for keeping her flying home all a secret and as everyone was hugging her and asking her questions, all I could think was how flipping enormous she'd got on her travels. Like she'd put on at least fifteen pounds! Maybe twenty. She looked like a lovely, cuddly, motherly version of my big sister.

"'Ere, I'll get you a drink!" said my mother. "What you want? A vodka lime and soda?"

"Ooh ... no Mum ... get me an orange juice," laughed Cava-Sue.

And then she looked at me and her cheeks went a bit pink, and I looked right back at her, right in her eyes. No one else had guessed, but I had. I'd guessed straight away.

So somehow I managed to whisk Cava-Sue into the ladies' loo and corner her by the paper towel dispenser and go, "OK, Cava-Sue, spill. You're up the duff! You're having a baby, aren't you! Don't say you're not, I know you are!" And she tries to pretend to look nonplussed and bewildered, but she can't fool me and she knows it, and she gives this funny, nervous laugh and she tells me, "Yes, I'm five months gone. Me? Shizza, I'm gonna be a mum, and you — you're gonna be an auntie."

And I look at her sort of amazed, and shocked, and happy and I say, "But how?! How are you pregnant?" And Cava-Sue says, "C'mon Shiz, you got all your GCSEs didn't you?!" And I say, "No, but how are YOU pregnant? You said this would never happen to you! You were proper outraged when folks like Collette Brown and Kezia Marshall got pregnant. You had dreams, you said. It wasn't going to happen to you, Cava-Sue Wood." So Cava-Sue looks at me and says, "Oh I know. I know. But the thing is then I met Lewis and he had all his own dreams. He wanted to give up studying and go traveling so I ended up doing that with him. And then I got bloody food poisoning in Vietnam and threw up my pills so they didn't work properly to stop me getting up the duff.

And when I told Lewis I thought he'd be really upset, but he was so happy, Shiraz! He said he couldn't wait to be a dad! He says he's always wanted to be a dad eventually, so why not now, eh? And I agree, why not now?"

I just looked at her and nodded and tried to look supportive but I felt, well, really, disappointed.

"That's the thing with boys, isn't it, Shiraz? You end up in so deep with them you start following their dream instead of your own. You'll get like that with your Wesley. It's your destiny," said Cava-Sue.

And then I knew. I knew I was going to London.

And before I could say anything else, my mother then ran into the ladies' loo looking like she'd just won the National Lottery shouting, "Oh my god! Have I just heard what I think I've heard, Cava-Sue?! My first grandchild! MY FIRST GRANDCHILD! THIS IS THE HAPPIEST DAY OF MY WHOLE LIFE."

By the time Mum and Cava-Sue had figured out how they'd fit Cava-Sue, Lewis, and a Moses basket into her old room, well, I'd already told Carrie that me and her would be needing to find a two-bedroom apartment far, far away from them all.

SATURDAY JULY 4TH

All told, Nan and Clement's wedding was lovely. Proper lovely.

If I ever get married, which won't be for a real long time, then I want it to be just like that. Obviously, not at Romford Registry Office and marrying an old geezer, no, but I want the room to feel like that when I walk up the aisle. Like everyone is totally happy for me and everyone can feel how much we're in love. Nan looked proper amazing in her cream suit from Marks and Spencer and her big cream hat. And Clement looked like a right old handsome bloke in his navy blue suit and dark gray fedora. And Murphy never lost the ring. And Mum never scared off Rema by asking when her and Murphy were getting hitched. And Dad only got a little bit drunk at the party and did his "Elvis on the toilet" impression once.

And Clement's toast was just perfect 'cos he said he wanted to be with Nan forever and he felt like his life began again when he saw her come into bingo at Chadwell Heath and he loved her with all his heart and soul. We were all nearly crying when he said that. And then everyone had a laugh and a drink and a dance and even more of a dance and eventually my feet began to hurt in my new shoes and Wesley saw I was knackered and he told Mum he'd take me home.

Wesley Barrington Bains II gave me a piggyback ride down the road from the social club in the moonlight. We both never said much all the way along the road, 'cos we both knew something was wrong between us and neither of us wanted to spoil the day. And eventually Wesley said, "So do you reckon that'll ever be me and you one day, innit?"

And I felt awful in my heart when he said that so I took a deep breath and said, "Well, if you want me to be proper honest, Wesley, no."

And then I told him about me and Carrie going to London. It felt like it would be properly tight if I never said anything right then. I explained it all in lots and lots of words about leaving Goodmayes and experiencing life and I tried my best to make him see.

And when I stopped talking he had tears in his eyes. And his bottom lip looked like he was having to try proper hard to stop it wobbling, 'cos he was trying to be tough like boys do and not let me see I'd broken his heart.

He wandered off into the moonlight down Thundersley Road and I watched his baggy silhouette until he turned the corner, then I went upstairs and got into bed and curled into a ball and cried.

MONDAY 6TH JULY

Well, what a weird day today has turned out to be.

Nothing like I'd figured it out.

I went round to Uma's and told her what I was up to and I'd expected her to be all "Whatever" but she wasn't, she was proper upset.

"Bloody hell, mate," Uma said, "Me and Zeus will miss you rotten, won't we, Zeus? What we going to do without Shiraz Bailey Wood? You're the only person in Essex that don't think I'm a one-woman crime wave!"

"No I'm not, Uma," I said. "Not anymore."

Uma says she'll come and visit me and Carrie in London. She says she's looking into training to be a dealer in a casino. Y'know something? I think she'll do OK.

The person I was really dreading telling was Ms. Bracket. I was proper bricking it as I knocked on her office door. Then she opened it with a big smile on her face and said, "So you've heard!" and I said, "Heard what?!" And she said, "You're talking to the new Mayflower Academy headmistress! Mr. Bamblebury has announced his retirement!" and I said, "Oh my God!!"

Of course, what I was going to tell her then seemed really bad. But she was sort of OK really. She listened proper carefully to what I said about my dreams, then she said, "Do you know, Shiraz, if you're so determined to see the world outside Goodmayes, I can't really stand in your way. But you know you can come back here and carry on with A2-Levels if it doesn't work out, don't you?"

"Can I?" I said.

And she looks at me and says, "Well, I suppose I can have a word with my boss . . . no, hang on . . . I am the boss! Yes! Of course I'll have you back. You're the legendary Shiraz Bailey Wood."

So I left Mayflower Academy and I went and met Carrie in Mr. Yolk. I walked through the door and Mario goes, "Hello, Shirelle! Your little friend with all the surprise eyes and mouth like a bee stung her face is here! She's in the corner!"

And there was Carrie, sitting with the newspaper, opened at the "Apartments for Rent" section going, " 'Ere Shiz, do you fancy Camden or Knightsbridge? North, south or central?" I grinned and sat down. Then my phone bleeped in my pocket.

It was a text message from Wesley Barrington Bains II. It said:

IF U NEED A LIFT WITH UR STUFF OR ANYTHING AT ALL — GIVE ME A SHOUT. I'LL ALWAYS BE HERE. W-B-B II XXX

I looked at it and my eyes began to sting a bit, but I pulled my-self together quickly.

"Oh, look at you two!" Mario was laughing, bringing us both a coffee. "Look at you, Shirelle! With all your gold on! Your hoops and your bracelets and your hoodie! You make me smile! You and your little friend! Always look like you're up to something! What you up to today then? Up to no bloody good!"

"You're not wrong, Mario," I said and took a swig of my coffee, got out a pen, and began circling ads for apartments.

I am the master of my own destiny, after all.

Hello Shirazheads in the United States of America!

'Ere, the lovely people at the publishing house have said I better explain some of the words I use in my diaries! They reckon I speak English, but just not English like anyone else they know does. Flaming cheek, eh?! Ha ha ha! So anyway, here's a few words to help you out. I hope this allows you to enjoy my books more 'cos to be totally honest I spent a whole night doing it when I could have been round Carrie's house eating noodles, getting my nails painted, and prank calling London Zoo, which we all know would have been way more fun. Keep it real blud!

Lots of love—Shizzlebizzlewoodxxxx

GLOSSARY

A-Level: (n.) Advanced level exams. Teenagers take these at 18 to qualify to go on to university. You can either leave school at 16 and work somewhere rubbish like a pot pie factory or make a choice to carry on in education and do your A-levels. But A-levels are really tough so only the nerds and swots end up doing them.

Agony Aunt: (n.) An Agony Aunt works on a magazine and you write to her with your "problems." She's meant to help you out, but in reality I reckon the work experience intern opens them and then everyone in the office has a laugh about your bum spots or the fact that your feet look a bit webbed. I would be an amazing Agony Aunt 'cos I always keep it real and people like to hear the truth, don't they?

'Arris: (n.) Bum, rear. See also: *jacksie.*

ASBO: (n.) Anti-social behavior order. The police give ASBOs to people to stop them causing trouble in a certain place. So if you always cause trouble in the park, your ASBO might forbid you visiting the park for 6 months. The Bruton-Fletchers have a LOT of ASBOs.

Baps: (n.) Boobs. Also boobies, breasts, blouse potatoes.

Bashment: (n.) A party.

Bint: (n.) An annoying woman. *"Ere I was standing in the line at KFC, right, and this BINT pushes in before me and orders a Bargain Bucket!"*

Boffin: (n.) Boffins are the people at school who always get straight A's and remember to bring their books and pens and know which class to be at on the right day and time. Their home-work never gets "stolen by a big dog" en route to school. When you ask a boffin what they want to do in the future they say, "I want to be a research scientist for NASA." They don't say, " 'Ere, come round my gaff at about seven, I'm prank calling the zoo pretending to be an escaped lion." Me and Carrie are not boffins.

Brassic: (adj.) Skint, penniless, broke, etc. *"Ere Shizzle, you coming to the mall on Saturday?"* *"Yeah, but mate I am totally brassic so I'll just be window shopping. I can't even afford any McNuggets."*

Bricking it: (vb.) Scared, nervous, so terrified you feel like you might have an accident in your thong. *"So, did you call dat hot boy on Saturday then?"* *"No, bruv, I was proper bricking it!"*

Buff: (adj.) Buff means a nice fit body. A hottie. *"Is he working out a lot? He is looking well buff."*

Butterz: (adj.) Ugly, minging, not attractive. Sort of "butt ugly" taken to the extreme. *"Don't let me snog Harry, even if I'm drunk right? He is well butterz!"*

Buzzing: (vb.) Feeling really excited.

Cark it: (vb.) 1: To die. *"He's off school. His gran carked it—he has to go to the funeral."* **2:** To stop working. *"OMG. We were halfway to Romford and Wesley's car totally carked it."*

Chas 'n' Dave: (n.) Terrible old-fashioned British music duo. One plays piano, one plays guitar. They both have beards. The sort of CD your mum and dad put on at New Year's after a few glasses of booze and start dancing to and you get seriously worried that one of them might slip and break a hip.

Chav: (n.) Chav is a not very nice word people often call me and my friends 'cos we wear hoodies and gold hoops and listen to R+B and own Staffordshire Bull Terriers and don't live in posh houses. People say chavs cause a lot of trouble. I don't think I am a chav, and if I am it stands for "charming, hilarious, articulate, and vibrant."

Choong: (adj.) Sexy, handsome, hottie. *"Oh my days, who is that new boy in class? He is proper choong, man, I can't stop staring!"*

Chuffed: (adj.) Happy, pleased. *"Awww, Wazzle is well chuffed, his ASBO doesn't stretch as far as Wembley Stadium so we can get tickets for Beyoncé!"* or *"Man, check out my new gold scunchy! Only a quid in Claire's Accessories. I am well chuffed!"*

Dossing: (vb.) To lie about doing nothing. *"I've been dossing about all day."*

Dubstep: (n.) A type of very fast British dance music that has to be played loud. The total opposite of Chas 'n' Dave. If you put this on in the car you can be sure your mother will be in a really bad mood when you get where you're going and will have pointed out at least once that there is "no tune" and she is "getting one of her migraines."

Earwigging: (vb.) Listening to something you ain't supposed to be. What mothers do when you're on the phone. Or when a boy you fancy walks past and you want to hear what he's saying.

EastEnders: (n.) A soap opera about London folk which plays three times a week on BBC1 in Britain. It is properly depressing but everyone is addicted to it.

Elizabeth Duke: (n.) Jewelry shop in Britain that posh people take the mickey out of 'cos it's not exactly Tiffany. *"OMG I love that diamond-covered clown-shaped pendant! Where'd you get that?"* *"My Wes got me it from Elizabeth Duke for Christmas!"*

Emmerdale: (n.) British soap opera that is on TV five times a week. It's set in a village in the countryside in Yorkshire, England. Everyone in Emmerdale has snogged each other or got divorced at least once and they argue about pigs and corn all the time. My mother likes *Emmerdale* a lot.

Faffing about: (vb.) Spending a lot of time very busily not achieving anything. *"Why are you late?!"* *"Oh god, sorry, I got up at seven*

AM and I've been faffing about ever since. I sort of started straightening my hair, then I started typing an e-mail, then I lost my keys and then I couldn't find a skirt and then one thing led to another and I decided to categorize my sock drawer into 'daywear,' 'fancy,' and 'sports/casual.'"

Fancy: (vb.) To have the hots for someone. *"I fancy him! I fancy him rotten!"*

Fangita: (n.) Lady-bits, front-bum, mimsy. *"I had to rearrange my thong, it was strangling my fangita!"* or *"We spent half an hour in biology looking at photos of fangitas. It proper put me off lunch, I can tell you."*

Fizzing: (adj.) Angry, irate.

Flog: (vb.) To sell something. *"I'm going to flog my bike, I need some cash."*

GCSE: (n.) The exam sixteen-year-olds take before they can choose to move on to A-Levels. Everyone who is sixteen in Britain takes GCSE exams. Then it's your choice whether you want to quit school FOREVER or study for some A-Levels, bearing in mind that studying for A-Levels will involve carrying on at school and being moaned at by teachers for another two years.

Geezer: (n.) A man, a bloke, a guy.

Git: (n.) Annoying person. *"He's such a total git sometimes! I said to him, 'Bruv, who's more buff, me or Beyoncé?' And he said Beyoncé!"* or *"OMG, this old git was in front of me in the supermarket queue taking ten hours to buy a tin of peaches and some false teeth glue."* See also: *bint.*

Gob: 1. (n.) Mouth 2. (adj.) To spit. *"He walked into class and gobbed his chewing gum on the floor! Ugh!"*

To get the hump: (vb.) To take offense. *"So she says to me, ''Ere, was that dress on sale in Top Shop or something 'cos it well looks cheap?' Well I proper got the hump, I did!"*

Grass: 1. (vb.) To tell the police/teachers/someone's parents about someone. Nark, tattle, sing, tell, spill, squeal. *"I had no choice mate, I had to grass her up!"* 2. (n.) a narc.

Hacked off: (adj.) Annoyed. *"Is that lovebite on your neck from my Trevor?! OMG I am TOTALLY HACKED OFF!"*

Headbend: (n.) Something so weird it makes you think your head is tripping out. *"What? The most gorgeous boy in the whole school has said he thinks I'm hot? OMG what a head bend!"*

Hen party: (n.) A party before a wedding for all the bride's friends where alcohol is consumed and women tend to get a bit rowdy and dress up in silly costumes and sometimes a stripper appears. This is in preparation for the time after your marriage when you sit about in a cardigan watching *Emmerdale.*

Hoodie: (n.) A hooded sweatshirt or sports top. The British are obsessed with hoodies and think that if kids wear them with the hood up it means they're a criminal. LMAO. "Hoodie" has now come to mean "kid who causes trouble," i.e., *"I'll tell you who I reckon stole my car stereo. It'll be those HOODIES from down the road who hang out by the chicken shop!"*

Jacksie: (n.) Ass, rear end. *"I ain't going to karaoke with Carrie no more. She sings six Mariah Carey songs in a row and chucks a diva-fit if you touch the microphone. What a pain in the jacksie she is."*

Jog on: (vb.) Get lost, go away, buzz off. *"He came over here trying to hit on me. I said, 'Jog on bruv, no chance.'"*

Khazi: (n.) Toilet, loo, lavatory. *"Yes mother, me and Wes were supposed to be going out for pizza, but don't worry, he'd LOVE to spend the night with his head down our khazi poking it with a spanner working out why it ain't flushing. No, really. No, I ain't being sarcastic."* or *"Where's Dad?" "Oh, he's on the khazi, he's been there an hour. He reckons it's the only place where he can get any peace."*

Knackered: (adj.) To be tired, shattered, exhausted.

Knob: (n.) A penis. But it's an insult too. *"Stop being a knob!"*

Lairy: (adj.) In the mood for fighting. Aggressive.

Liberty: 1. (n.) Someone who is really cheeky and just does whatever she wants. *"She is a right liberty, she is."* **2.** Someone who takes liberties.

Merk: (vb.) Kill, murder. *"OMG, that's another kid on the news got merked on Saturday night. Someone shot him."*

Modded car: (n.) When you take a normal car and make it unique by sticking and gluing bits to it and changing the wheel trims and putting lights on it and installing a proper loud stereo. My Wes has a modded banana yellow Volkswagen Golf, which is proper brilliant. Modding a car is just like on *Pimp My Ride*, except there, they get proper professionals to make the car look amazing and the owner always cries with happiness—unlike when Bezzy Kelleher starts the fake fog machine on his Vauxhall Nova and people basically cry with laughter.

Mush: (n.) Mouth, gob. *"Oi! Shut your mush!"*

Munter: (n.) Ugly, minging, not hot. *"I thought I'd pulled a right hottie at that party . . . then the lights went on, and I was like, 'What a munter!'"*

Narky: (adj.) In a bad mood. Takes offense easily.

Nicking: (vb.) Stealing, thieving.

Norks: (n.) Knockers. Also: boobs, boobies, norkers, norgs, norgers. See also: *baps.*

NVQ: (n.) National Vocational Qualification. An exam you take in Britain instead of your A-Levels specifically to get a job like a plumber or an electrician.

Pearly king: (n.) Old British person from East London who turns up on special occasions in a jacket and hat covered in about a million white buttons. It's like a special tradition dating back from Ye Olde times of England when poor London folk had no TV or Playstations or R+B to listen to so they spent the long nights waiting to die from smallpox and sewing buttons onto their clothes and thinking it made them look fancy like the real royal family. My Nan loves pearly kings and her eyes all light up when you mention them, but she once got tipsy and told me she'd snogged one at a party in 1950 and was shaking buttons out of her undergarments for the next week.

Pikey: (n.) A not very nice slang word for a gypsy or basically anyone who looks a bit poor. Real pikeys live in trailers and get hassled by the government for not paying taxes. I often used to tell our Murphy that his real family were pikeys 'cos it used to make him cry. Sorry, Murph.

Right hump: (n.) To totally take offense about something. See also: *get the hump.*

Row: (n.) An argument, a spat. *"Wesley and Bez are having a right old row out there! Bezzy got McDonald's barbecue sauce all down Wesley's new car seat covers. He's going mental!"*

Rude: (n.) Someone who thinks they're tough or a bit of a gangster. Often combined with *girl* or *boy*: *"She acts like she's a rudegirl, but she ain't all that."*

Scrounging: (vb.) Begging.

Shubz: (n.) A party, a knees-up, a gathering. *"Leticia is having a shubz on Saturday night when her mum and dad are out. Everyone is invited! You coming?"* *"Nah, mate, I'll just read the police report afterward in the* Ilford Bugle.*"*

Sixth Form: (n.) A school where you go to study your A-Levels that is often in the same school where you took GCSE's. Basically it is a building full of boffins and school nerds who actually learn things for their own pleasure and want to be brain surgeons and who know all the capitals of the world and crap about the Ice Age and stuff (i.e., not me at all).

Skiving: (vb.) Bunking off, skipping off when you haven't got a good excuse.

Skunk: (n.) A type of grass or marijuana.

Slapper: (n.) A girl who is very well known to the boys in the local area due to her, ahem, friendly and outgoing nature. *"Pghgh, no wonder he's started going out with Suzanne, she's a right slapper."*

Snog: (vb., n.) An open-mouthed kiss, which may or may not include tongues. I once snogged Carlton Brown behind a bush after a Year eight disco and he bit my face by accident and his breath smelled of Big Mac gherkins. It was proper disgusting.

Sovereign ring: (n.) A ring that you might buy from somewhere like Elizabeth Duke. It looks like it is made from an old fashioned British sovereign gold coin.

Spots: 1: (n.) Zits. Red lumps full of pus that appear on your face the day before a party and make you look like a freak. Also: *spotty* (adj.).

Staffy: (n.) Staffordshire Bull Terrier. A dog that a lot of chavs own. Oh, and the Wood family owns one too, called Penny, but as I say, we aren't chavs!

Stroppy: (adj.) Sulky, in the mood to throw a hissy fit. Also: *stroppiest* (adj.) and *strop* (n.). *"She gave me her stroppiest look when she saw I looked better in that dress than she did!"*

Sucking teeth: (vb.) Some people suck their teeth to let you know they're not happy with you. *"I said to her, 'Are both those seats taken* *or is your ass just so wide it's spilling onto the second one?' But she just sucked her teeth and turned her head."*

Take the mickey: (vb.) To make fun of someone or have a joke with them. Taking the mickey can be nice or not nice, depending on how far you take it. Like I take the mickey out of my Carrie a lot for being so vain. But Latoya Bell is just plain unpleasant when she takes the mickey. In fact, she's just a bully. Also: *take the piss.*

Tight: (adj.) Mean. *"I've been really taking the mickey about his new haircut. Okay, I know I'm being a bit tight."*

Trackie: (n.) Track suit or sweat suit.

Up the duff: (n.) Pregnant, knocked up, in the pudding club. *"OMG, I saw Katy drinking vodka outside Perfect Chicken and she is totally up the duff too!"*

WAG: (n.) British Football term meaning "Wives and girlfriends," i.e., the women who turn up to games to support their husbands/ boyfriends dressed in $50,000 of designer gear and get drunk on champagne and snog other footballers that aren't their boyfriends, then end up on the front of *The Sun* newspaper falling out of a nightclub being sick in their $5000 Miu Miu handbags.

Well minted: (adj.) To have lots of cash. *"Have you seen his car? Man, he must be well minted I reckon!"*

Wide: (adj.) Dodgy, shady, dishonest. *"I wouldn't lend him money if I were you, he can be a bit wide sometimes."*

Wiffling on: (vb.) Yaddering, chattering, blathering. *"I thought my class speech was going so well. But then I got distracted and started wiffling on for half an hour about my favorite sandwich. OMG, epic fail."*

Welcome to Poppy.

A poppy is a beautiful blooming red flower
(like the one on the spine of this book). It is also
the name of the home of your favorite books.

Poppy takes the real world and makes it
a little funnier, a little more fabulous.

Poppy novels are wild, witty, and inspiring.
They were written just for you.

So sit back, get comfy, and pick a Poppy.

www.pickapoppy.com

THE A-LIST
HOLLYWOOD ROYALTY

gossip girl

THE CLIQUE

ALPHAS

SECRETS OF MY
HOLLYWOOD LIFE

the it girl

POSEUR